COWBOY
BIKERS MC

COWBOY
BIKERS MC #7

By Esther E. Schmidt

COWBOY
BIKERS MC

Cover design by:

Esther E. Schmidt

Editor #1:

Christi Durbin

Editor #2:

Virginia Tesi Carey

DEDICATION

"The past is something no one can change.
The future, though?
Wide open. Remember that."

CHAPTER 01

GARRETT

"Care to explain why you bought that horse? You do know we breed damn fine ones ourselves, right?" Oak, one of my brothers, questions.

I shrug and keep up my pace. "Saddle breaking age, nice bloodline, and the mare was totally calm, even with the sound of a truck backfiring."

"True, but still–"

"Give it up, Oak. My money, my decision. Hell, if you don't stop nagging like a bitch, I might get the feeling you're pissed I got myself a sweet deal, one you wanted instead. Besides, we sold the three horses we brought, club business is done, and we have an empty trailer going home. I might as well take advantage and get myself a new mare." I slap Oak on the back. "Be a good pal and help a brother out by getting my horse into the trailer while I handle the rest of the paperwork."

"Fine, but you're driving home so I can sleep," Oak grumbles.

I wave my hand in the air as I walk away from him. I don't mind driving the six hours back home. I've never been one who needs loads of sleep anyway. I'm up at the crack of dawn even if I only had my eyes closed for four hours.

Hard work and dedication provide the kind of satisfaction you need to fuel your will to live another day. It also gives you the opportunity to reap the fruits of your labor, and that's what I'm doing today; buying a horse as a present to myself.

Like Oak mentioned, I could have my pick from the horses owned and bred by the club, but it's different. Something about the easy road giving less resistance. While now I'm getting myself a horse I haven't bred, raised, or trained.

And there's something about this mare. She caught my eye when they brought her into the auction. I was about to turn away and head home but the Palomino stood out with her gold coat and white mane. Add the serenity of her presence and it triggered possibilities inside my head to train her as my main horse to both work with while herding livestock but also enjoy early morning rides.

You can clearly see someone gave this horse love while she was growing up. I get the feeling this mare is worth every penny I just paid. The paperwork is handled quickly and I'm walking back to the trailer when I notice a small commotion.

Oak has his arms crossed in front of his chest and is blocking the entrance of the trailer as if he needs to guard it. I can clearly see the mare is loaded up and the way Oak is now pointing at it and leaning into the tiny person in front of him, I'd say the commotion is about the horse.

"What's going on?" I rumble and come to a stop behind the woman who is facing a man twice her size.

She spins around and lets her gaze collide with mine. And damn does it collide. It's more of a full front collision with lust sparking on impact. The brightest of green eyes, high cheekbones, puffy lips, and the fire in her gaze is most definitely intriguing to say the least. And all of it is framed by long black hair. Fucking stunning.

"This man here is taking my horse," she says and jabs her finger against Oak's chest.

Shit. Talk about a missed chance to act on the whole sparking lust thing I just experienced because we're about to face off.

Now I'm the one crossing my arms in front of my chest when I tell her, "I bought this horse at the auction. She's mine, everything is in order."

"Everything is *not* in order," she hisses with a slight tremor in her voice and steps closer.

I now notice how her face is showing a hint of despair. She's either not used to standing up to someone or this is a matter of the heart with the way emotions are slicing through her eyes.

I soften my voice and tell her, "I can show you the papers."

"That won't be necessary. Don't mind my daughter, she's overdramatic." I turn to face the man who rumbled out the words and watch how his face turns into a menacing glare as his tone hardens when he tells the woman, "Get your ass away from those men and into the truck, girl. We're leaving."

Girl? She might not be wearing any make up and is tiny as fuck, but he's talking to his daughter as if she's twelve while I'm pretty damn sure she's a grown-ass woman.

"No." The word might be a denial coming from her lips but the two letters are on a breath laced with a hint of fear.

I tear my gaze away from the man and assess

the woman who has her hands turned into fists–knuckles white–while she waits for her father to respond. And the way she's bracing herself lets me know the man has a track record of talking to his daughter by using his hands.

"Ass. In. The. Truck." The man spits out his words one by one and each of those make her fucking flinch.

There's clearly something going on between these two. I step in front of her and face the man.

"Mind explaining why she thinks I'm taking her horse?" I calmly ask.

"No need." The man reaches around me to grab the woman by the arm and pulls her forward. "This one's always been on the stupid and crazy side. Thanks for the sale. Have a safe ride home."

He starts to drag her away but she rips her arm from his grip. She shoves her hand into the back pocket of her ragged jeans and holds out a rumpled piece of paper for me to take.

"My father sold her to me before she was born.

I've worked my entire life at the ranch without asking for one damn thing and I've earned her by doing extra chores. I paid for her with hard work. He wrote a contract. See? You can't take her, she's mine." Every word tumbling from her cherry-colored lips is one of despair and it slices through my damn chest.

I take the paper from her and let the words of her so-called contract sink in. It takes everything inside me to stay rooted and not punch this fucker in the face. Keeping my anger at bay I shove the paper into my pocket.

The man has the nerve to smirk and give me the words, "Kids. Always a fucking pain in the ass. As you can *read*." He slides his attention from me to his daughter. "There is no issue. My daughter and I are going to take a little walk. Raney. Come here."

Instead of taking a step toward her father she backs up closer to Oak and gets behind me. I have to give it to her, from what I'm experiencing in this moment there are a few things very fucking clear. One, I'm almost positive the woman can't read. And two, she's not as stupid as her father thinks she is.

"Raney," I address her but keep my eyes on her father. "Instead of taking a little walk with your father, would you mind having a little chat with me in private?"

"Not going to happen," her father snaps.

I put a load of steel in my voice when I tell the asshole, "Not your call cause for damn sure it's going to happen. And if it's not? It won't be because you're throwing out demands but about the fucking fact that the lady has a choice. Now, Raney, can I talk to you about our horse?"

The timid "yes," flowing through the air behind me is enough for me to slightly turn and face Oak.

"Keep an eye on things, brother." I don't have to ask him to have my back.

We're both members of the Iron Hot Blood MC. A solid brotherhood located on a ranch where we breed and train horses along with other livestock.

"I said," the woman's father starts but Oak is stepping toward him.

I take the woman's hand and guide her around the trailer to create some distance and privacy.

As soon as we're out of earshot from her father she asks with a tremor in her voice, "What did the note say? It wasn't a contract, was it?"

As I figured; pretty sure she can't read.

"How old are you?" I question, needing to know this for what I'm about to do next.

"Twenty-one." Her eyes are searching mine. "Why?"

"You're right. The paper you gave me wasn't a contract."

Her shoulders sag and she looks as if life itself just shattered in front of her. "Figures."

"I have no clue about your situation, but if I had to guess it's not good. So, I'm going to offer you something, okay?"

Her eyes find mine and she tilts her head. "Offer me something?"

I tap my finger on the patch of my leather cut. "I'm a biker but our MC is located at a ranch. I have a small cabin with a spare bedroom I'm offering to you. No strings attached. You can get on your feet, away from your father, whatever. I'll even pay you if you want to take care of the horse. I wasn't planning on buying a horse today since we train and breed horses ourselves. But I recognize a good horse when I see one. That being said, I have my own work to do and could use the help. So, what do you say? Free room and board, earning some cash and stay with your horse while you're at it."

"She's my horse," she fucking croaks and might as well rip my heart out along with it.

"Like I said, come along and I'll give you a job. Hell, I'll throw in the option to buy her back while you get your shit together. Deal?"

She narrows her eyes. "Are you going to give

me a real contract?"

"Yes, you have my word," I reply through clenched teeth. "One thing I will never do is lie."

Her head tilts. "I should question whether or not you're a con-artist, a serial killer, or a rapist, but I guess it's a chance I have to take."

"Fucking hell," I grumble underneath my breath and take off my Stetson to run my fingers over the buzzcut I'm sporting before answering. "I'm none of those things. And for you to add it's a chance you have to take? Woman, for you to say that shit makes me fucking angry."

She flinches and blurts, "I'm sorry."

I have to inhale deep and slowly let that shit out because my anger is all-consuming. She's apologizing for the bad situation she's in–and for my anger due to all of it–while nothing is her fault.

Deciding not to dwell and move forward, I throw out the question, "Do you need to go home and get a few things?"

She looks down at herself and shrugs. "I only

have one other pair of clothes. If I earn money by working for you, I can buy some new ones. Till then I can wash these before I go to sleep and have them dry by morning."

One pair of... another deep breath and I manage a few more when I really take in the woman standing before me. She owns a single change of clothes, is tiny as fuck, and has minimal meat on her bones but still stands strong as if she can handle a heavy load. I'd say she's been working her ass off all her life for nothing more than one meal a day.

"Hungry?" Shit. I keep asking her question after question.

She bites her bottom lip. "I could eat."

"I bet you could," I mutter. "I gather we have a deal then?"

She quickly nods and holds out her hand. "We have a deal if you give me a job and Izzy back."

"Izzy?"

"Our horse." She gives me a shy smile.

"Our horse," I echo. "You move in with me, work for the cash I'll pay you for taking care of Izzy, and I'll give you the promise she'll be yours soon enough."

"Soon enough," she murmurs.

I take her hand and it's the same as when our eyes collided the first time; an explosion of lust slams into me. Into the both of us if I can judge by the sharp gasp tumbling over her lips and how her pupils dilate.

Not something we need in this moment and it's for this reason I tell her, "Get in the truck, front seat. I'm driving and Oak will be in the back seat."

Her head bobs and she walks around the truck to get in while I head for the back of the trailer. Before I reach it, Oak steps out from behind the trailer.

"Ready to go?" he questions.

I look past him. "Yeah. Where did her father go?"

"I told him to piss the fuck off. She's coming

with us I assume?"

"Yeah," I repeat. "The fucker left without so much as a peep?"

Oak rubs two fingers against his jaw while his upper lip twitches in anger. "Not so much as one. I might have punched him once in the face and threatened to gut him if he didn't get the fuck out of my sight. I might not know what the hell is going on between the father and your girl, but even a blind man can see that shit ain't pretty. What did the note say? The one she gave you?"

Your girl. Those words roll easy over his tongue. Just as easy as they sound damn right in my ears, and I barely know the girl who I met mere minutes ago. But like hell am I ever going to share with anyone what was written on the damn note.

"It doesn't matter." I smack his upper arm. "Thanks, man. I owe you one for getting rid of the fucker. Come on, let's head home."

"Sounds good," Oak grunts and gets into the back of the truck. I make one final round to check if everything is okay with the trailer and my new horse before I get behind the wheel and head home.

I for sure didn't expect to return home with a new horse, let alone bring a woman back to my cabin along with it. But it seems life has a way of throwing things in your path when you least expect it. And to say I'm intrigued by both animal and woman is an understatement.

I can't wait to get to know the both of them. The horse might have to wait but I'm spending the next couple of hours with the woman sitting right next to me. So, I guess it'll be a crash course getting to know her since I kinda lied about having a spare room.

Hopefully she doesn't mind sharing a bed, otherwise I'll be sleeping on the couch in my own damn house. But I guess that's the angle of shit thrown in your path when you least expect it. And sleeping on the couch or not, I know I did the right thing by offering her a way out. The damn note is still branded inside my head.

I am such a dumb fuck, I can't even read.
If I could, I would know this note is a load
of bullshit. Nothing is promised and
nothing is owned. I am stupid
and I will never achieve anything.
I will keep working for my father
for as long as I live.
My name is Raney and I'm an idiot.

The note is clearly written and signed by her father. I recognize the signature I just saw on the property papers of the horse. Wiley Bolcord. Fucking asshole. How the hell can you call yourself a father when you degrade your own daughter like that?

My knuckles are white as I grip the wheel. It's a good thing Oak handled her father because thinking this shit through…I would have done more than punch the fucker in the face and tell him to get the fuck out of my sight.

"You okay, dude?" Oak questions from the back seat.

"Fine," I grunt.

Oak snorts. "Sure you are. Okay you two, I'm gonna sleep for a few hours. Wake me up if you stop to eat something, otherwise don't wake me unless we're back home."

I give another grunt and watch through the rearview mirror how he settles in before I let my gaze slide back to the road in front of me. Silence hits the truck and to be honest? I need it to let my thoughts settle.

Glancing beside me I get a hint of the woman's profile. She's wearing a tiny smile and has her hands folded on her lap. I would like to know what she's thinking. She doesn't seem scared or sad. To be honest it looks like she's hopeful.

Fucking hell, for a young woman to be hopeful while she just left her father, twenty-one years old with no possessions, sitting in a truck with two complete strangers while she agreed to come with me…to my house…promises that might as well be lies to fuck her over.

Yeah. Desperate situations call for desperate decisions and choices taken with your back against the wall. No fucking wonder she's hopeful. And it makes the need inside me rise to make sure this woman gets everything she desires and more.

But I guess I have to tackle the little lie I told her first…about the spare room…all while I mentioned to her I never lie. We're already off to a good fucking start.

CHAPTER 02

RANEY

My heart is pounding in my chest, each beat fills my body with a fragment of hope. Hope for a better future. *Any type of future as long as it's different from my past.* But mostly one where I have a space for me and my horse. That's all I ask. I don't need much. Not to mention, I've slept in the stable for as long as I can remember.

I've never had a lot, never complained, and work hard to keep the stress and aggravation to a minimum. Keep your head down and get through the day meant spending the night with my horse for the past three years. Only to find out my father lied once more and betrayed me.

I shake my head in an effort to clear my thoughts. I want to leave it behind me. I should. I'm in a truck with two strangers but also with the one thing I love more than my own life; my horse. She's in the trailer and I'm thankful for the man driving the truck to allow me the chance to hopefully have the future I desire.

Glancing over my shoulder I try to keep my laughter at bay when I see the awkward position Oak is sagged into while he's snoring loud. I shake my head and shift to look out the front window again.

I blurt out my thoughts, "He's going to wake up with a sore neck."

Garrett glances in the rearview mirror and back to the road in front of him. "Nah. We have these kind of road trips every once in a while and the idiot always sleeps like that. You can say he's used to it, or he just doesn't complain about being a human pretzel when he wakes up."

I risk a quick glance at Garrett. He introduced himself and Oak when we were a few minutes into the drive. Garrett Verhams. A name I won't simply forget. He not only bought the horse I loved even before she was born, but he also stood up for me. Something no one has ever done.

There has been one other moment in my life where a guy should have stood up to my father and helped me, but the guy in question zipped-up his pants and ran. Though getting caught in the barn after having sex with the son of one of my father's men wasn't as humiliating as what I experienced when Garrett discovered I couldn't read the note I handed him.

Embarrassment hits me again and his reaction makes me more ashamed due to not knowing what was written on the note. There were complete sentences on it and it looked like a contract of sorts because I did recognize my own name and my father signed it; I've seen him place his signature a load of times. Here I thought he wrote down how Izzy belonged to me.

Gathering mental strength, I ask with a very thin voice, "Please tell me what was on the note."

He gives a curt shake of his head. "It's not important."

"It is to me. I want to know," I press.

"How about this…I'll teach you how to read so it won't happen again."

"I'd rather have you read it to me," I grumble and turn my head to face the side window to add underneath my breath what my parents told me many times, "Besides, the reason I can't read is because I'm too stupid to learn."

"What the fuck, woman?" Garrett snaps. "No one is too stupid to learn."

"I am." I can clearly hear the words echo inside my head from both my mother and my father telling me repeatedly I'm only capable of working with my hands. "You don't know me. But no worries, what my head can't learn, I'm more than able to make up for with my hands. I can work. No reading necessary."

"I might not know you but I know people. You can learn anything you want as long as you want it badly enough. It's all about the effort you or any-one else around you are willing to help out with. No matter how slow or fast, taking one step after another is moving forward. And some might in-deed not be able to study or become something out of their reach, but everyone has their own qualities in life. That's why there are many jobs and profes-sions."

My cheeks heat from shame. I would love to be able to read but this man already offered to help me in other ways, I can't be a more of a burden than I already am. "I'd rather work with my hands. I love animals, so no worries about helping me to learn how to read. You have your job and I'll work for you. See? No reading required."

"What if I hand you a list of things I need you

to do?" he easily replies.

A sigh rips from me. "You can tell me, I have a good memory."

There's a smile in his voice when he replies. "See? You're smart. So, don't ever let me hear you calling yourself stupid or dumb ever again, understood?"

"You can be very annoying," I mutter.

A chuckle flows through the truck and my eyes are instantly drawn to him. His jaw is smooth and nicely shaven. The leather Stetson he had on earlier–which showed years of wear but it adds to its character–is now off for the drive and shows the man has a short buzzcut.

The broad shoulders and thick, muscled forearms give the impression he's strong and most definitely doesn't have a desk job. The roughness of his hands and fingers also shows this man works with his hands. One hand is covered with a tattoo, going up and underneath his sleeve and I wonder how far it travels up.

"I am," Garrett says and pulls me from my ogling moment. "And I'm pretty sure we're going to get a crash course getting to know one another since we'll be living together for the time being. And...I might as well tell you I kinda lied earlier. I know I said I wouldn't lie and I didn't exactly lie."

I turn slightly in my seat to face him. Dread fills me and I push out the words as my heart starts to slam against my rib cage, "You're not going to let me earn Izzy back?"

"What?" he grunts. "No. That's not it. I lied about having a spare room. I only have my bed-room so we either have to share a bed or I'll crash on the couch."

Relief washes through me. "Oh, thank heav-ens. You scared me there. No worries about my sleeping arrangements, I'd be happy to sleep in the stable with Izzy. I actually prefer it since I've al-ways done so."

"Always...fucking hell. I keep repeating your words when you spew things that shock the fuck out of me. You know it's not normal to sleep with your horse, right? I mean, once or twice for fun or if we have a mare who's close to giving birth–" A strangled growl rumbles from his chest. "From now on things will be different."

He presses a few buttons and I hear a call connect through the speakers.

"Hey Cassidy," Garrett quips.

"Hey yourself, are you guys on your way back?" a female named Cassidy asks in a sweet and kind tone.

A burst of jealousy hits me and I have no clue why because Garrett isn't mine. I hardly know him or the woman. Shit. I just assumed he didn't have a girlfriend. Maybe he's married, has a handful of kids, who knows.

"We'll be home within a few hours, but could you do me a favor?"

"I'm not cooking anything and neither are the other old ladies," the woman huffs and I have to bite my lip not to laugh when I see Garrett rolling his eyes.

"It's not about food," Garrett grumbles. "I'm bringing a woman with me."

"Ooooohhh. Seriously? Wait. Don't tell me it's a mare or I'll kick your ass. You're talking about one with breasts and who can really talk and walk, a human woman, right?"

Now I can't help but bark out a laugh and quickly slam a hand over my mouth to cover the sound.

Garrett glares at me for a breath or two and drags his gaze back to the road as he answers, "Actually, I've found myself two women, Cassidy. And I can ride them both, but the one with the stunning rack and two sexy legs she walks on is why I'm calling."

I instantly choke and start to cough.

"She's there? She heard...dude, not nice. And why are you calling? Oh, hey, Garrett's woman. I'm Cassidy, his VP's old lady."

I remove my hand from my mouth and take a

calming breath. "Hi, Cassidy. I'm Raney."

"Don't you sound like a sweet thang. Can't wait to meet you."

"Yeah, yeah. Can you get her a few things? It was a spur of the moment thing for her to come with me and she didn't have time to pack a bag so a change of clothes would be nice."

"I'll call the other old ladies and we will organize a little something, no worries. It's going to be a few hours until you get here, yes?"

"Yes, but I'll get her whatever she needs tomorrow…for now she just needs some things to–"

"Shush, Garrett, we got this. See you later." The woman simply hangs up on him.

I have no clue who she is but she sounds sweet and like a good friend.

Many questions rise inside my head but the one I would like to know the answer to the most is the first I blurt without thinking, "Do you have a girlfriend?"

He doesn't glance my way when he answers.

"I wouldn't have offered you to stay with me if I did. And most definitely wouldn't have mentioned sharing a bed."

"What's a VP's old lady?"

"I'm a member of the Iron Hot Blood MC. Like I mentioned, we live on a ranch and all work together. Cassidy is my vice president's old lady. My VP is Roper. He's claimed Cassidy, she's his woman and with it protected by the club. You can compare it to getting married...biker style. My president is Weston and his old lady is Harlene. Decker has an old lady too, Muriel. And then there's Ledger, his old lady is Mayven. And you're also going to meet Kadence, Cold's old lady. And let's not forget Greta, she belongs to both Alfie and Joaquin. But I'm sure the old ladies will fill you in soon enough with all the details and the dynamics of the club."

I try to process everything he said and all the names he threw out. I know a ranch is a lot of work and no one can manage it alone, it's why my father always had a few men around to help him and why I was always working my ass off.

But there's one thing he just mentioned that stands out. "Greta has two men?"

Garrett snickers. "Caught that didn't you? No worries, like I said, the old ladies will fill you in soon enough."

My curiosity spikes. I've always been a person who asks too many questions, or so my parents always told me. Over time I've learned how to either keep them to myself or find the answer another way. But it seems Garrett doesn't mind if I fire one question after another.

The hours quickly pass through our easy chit-chat and before I know it my nerves spike when Garrett brings the truck to a stop at a huge ranch. Night has fallen but that doesn't take away the beauty of it. Horses and Longhorns are grazing in different pastures, lit by the moonlight it's rather captivating to take in the amazing view.

"Gorgeous," I gasp and open the truck door.

"Rise and shine, Oak, we're here," Garrett snaps and slams the door shut behind him.

I stroll over to one of the pastures and lean my forearms on the fence.

"I'll show you around in the morning," Garrett says as he comes to a stop next to me. "Want to help get Izzy settled in?"

I give him a radiant smile. "Yes. Stable or pasture?"

"Stable. She can take the one next to the other two horses I own."

Confused I step back. "You have more horses? Why did you buy Izzy?"

He places a hand on my lower back and guides me toward the trailer. "One of mine, Cal, is twenty-one and I don't want him to do the hard work anymore. I also have Kayla, she's sixteen, but when I saw Izzy I kinda wanted a horse for myself to enjoy besides work. And while Cal is enjoying her somewhat retirement, I'd like for him to have a buddy. I noticed Izzy not just because of her beauty but also the calmness of her character."

"Where I was thankful to have one horse, you now have three…such luxury," I blurt and realize it's none of my business and quickly add, "You are right about Izzy, she'd make a great buddy for Cal. She's calm by nature but she's used to a lot since I've always had her trail along with me every second I could."

Garrett smiles. "How does that work, the trail along part?"

"Izzy's mom died. My father didn't want to spend the money on a vet but the men who work for him guessed it was either a tear of the uterine artery, causing a small leak,   or an infection, or both for that matter. Thankfully Izzy did get a good start with the colostrum and we had another mare who gave birth a day before Izzy was born who somewhat adopted her. Izzy and I have spent every day together ever since. Me fixing fences… her darting around me, cleaning stables, her darting around me. Helping out with training horses, she'd be by my side. She's actually crazy enough to want a scarf around her neck when it's snowing."

I shoot him a grin at the reminder and realize I might come across as a stupid kid, making the happiness instantly fall flat.

"Mind sharing why the drop in happiness?" the observant man questions.

Remembering his mention of not to call myself stupid, I might as well keep it vague instead of lying because I can't let him know I value his opinion. Not only because I'm thankful for him stepping up for me, but mainly since I think he's insanely sexy. And I'm feverishly attracted to him. But dreams are like a puff of steam; semitransparent and easily evaporated.

I've never allowed myself to dream. And it's not like Garrett would see something in me as a woman to build a future with. I mean, he owns three horses and a cabin and works at this gorgeous ranch and has a group of friends. And then there's me, owning only the clothes I'm wearing.

Shit. I just met the man and my issues are piling up. This morning when my father and I left for the auction I didn't have any issues going through my head. All I did was work and sleep, day in, day out.

I thought we were headed to the auction to sell two horses. When we arrived, my father sent me to handle something. I didn't even find out my father had brought Izzy until I saw her standing in the ring, sold off without a second thought.

"Raney." Garrett's voice draws me back to the here and now.

A burst of female chatter rings out and six women and a man come strolling our way. All gorgeous with curves, unlike me. I'm more boyish and a stick-like figure. Yeah, dreams about having a future with the man who is looking intently at me are going to stay dreams for sure.

CHAPTER 03

GARRETT

Raney is clearly not used to attention from other women. Her eyes hold slight panic and she's wringing her hands while half of the time her head bobs in answer instead of giving them actual words.

I left her with the old ladies for the time it took me to put Izzy into the stable. The second I knew she was settled I headed back out and found Raney still rooted in the spot where I left her. Taking the bag Cassidy has beside her, I swing it over my shoulder and hold out my hand for Raney to take.

"Thanks, girls. Appreciate y'all coming out to welcome Raney and get her a few things, but we're gonna head for the cabin now. Catch ya later, tomorrow or whenever 'cause Raney is going to be here for a while. It's been a long day and I'm sure she wants to see where our horse is staying."

Raney slides her hand in mine.

"*Our horse?* As in yours and hers? How did that happen? Or did you buy one and got one free?" Kadence snickers.

I can feel Raney tense up, her cheeks heat and I can practically read the embarrassment in her eyes.

"All you need to know is that the mare belongs to both me and Raney and that Raney needed a job and I offered her one along with a place to stay. Like I said, it's been a long day."

The girls complain against our backs but I couldn't care less and drag her away to head for the stables.

46

"I figured you wanted to see how Izzy is doing before we take care of you."

She mindlessly nods as her eyes widen. Her head whips around to take in the stables.

"I'm guessing you like Izzy's new home?" I give a low chuckle because I'm stating the obvious.

"I don't think I could ever clean my parents' house as clean as this place," she muses.

Her answer strikes me as odd and I can't help but question, "How about your home? Did you live with your parents? Have your own space?"

She rolls her eyes. "My home was the barn: it was anything except clean."

My chest squeezes when I see her wince from blurting the truth. Her gaze hits the ground and I'm not liking the way she hides herself from me.

Tipping her chin up to force her to look into my eyes I tell her, "The past is something no one can change. The future, though? Wide open. Remember that."

Her throat bobs and her voice is paper thin when she whispers, "But I don't have anything, what kind of future do I have?"

"One where someone gives you a chance, an opportunity. You already grabbed it with both hands. So, I fucking say you have a future. The rest is up to you."

Gratitude washes over her face and she surprises me when she grabs my leather cut and lifts herself on her toes. Reality sets into my brain at super speed and I for sure as fuck don't want a peck on the cheek, putting me in the damn "friendzone."

Flashing my hand to the back of her neck, I curve her movements slightly and capture her mouth with mine. Yeah. Fuck friendzone. Life is too short for long runs and darting around shit. When I see something good, I tend to dive right in. And chatting with her for hours during the long ride home and the way electricity sparks between us? No way I'm passing up this opening shot.

The tiny gasp of surprise allows me to swoop

my tongue over her lips and taste her. At first, she's tentatively swirling her tongue against mine but when I squeeze her neck and shift the angle of her head to deepen the kiss, we go from soft to frantic.

Her hands slide over my chest and up to my head. I'm vaguely aware my Stetson falls off but her nails trailing over my scalp feels damn fantastic. Dropping the bag I was holding to free my hand, I instantly grab her ass and drag her against me, making sure she feels what one kiss from her does to me. She moans into my mouth and it spurs me on to kiss her harder.

"Look at that. Garrett, my man. Come home with not one nice lady but two, huh?" Alfie's words reluctantly force me to break the kiss.

I'm still holding her body tight with one hand cupping her neck and the other one possessively on her ass. Guiding her head into the crook of my neck, I keep her close and our connection vibrant when I answer Alfie.

"The horse belongs to both me and Raney. I'll introduce my woman to the club in the morning after we're settled and had a few hours of sleep. And if you'll excuse us, we're gonna check on Izzy real quick and head for my cabin right after."

Alfie snickers. "Anxious to get her alone, are you, eh? All right, I'll leave you two to it. I'm done with my chores for today and am itching to get home. I'm told there is a blow job in it for me from my man while eating my woman's pussy, ain't gonna pass it up just by talking to you guys. See you in the morning. Have a good night, I know I will."

He turns on his heel and walks out. I brace myself for Raney's reaction because Alfie doesn't have a damn filter. He also doesn't shy away to let everyone know he has both a woman and a man and how they are living happily together.

She's shaking as I pull her from the crook of my neck but when I check her gorgeous face, I see she has laughter written all over her. "That's the one you told me about? Who is in a relationship with another man along with a woman?"

"Yeah," I wince. "I should have given you a bit more of a heads up how Alfie blurts out whatever is on his mind. Needless to say, most times it's about sex."

A giggle slips over her full lips and it's cock-stroking. I need to focus. All I want to do is drop to my knees, rip off her pants, and lick her pussy to find out if she tastes as sweet as she seems.

"As long as the work gets done, who are we to judge what another person does?" The twinkle in her eyes shows she's still laughing on the inside but her attention is drawn to Izzy.

I scoop up my Stetson and put it on while we stroll closer. The horse is eating some hay and seems completely at ease. We take a few minutes to watch Izzy until Raney finally says, "I could use a shower and a nap. With getting everything set, the long drive to the auction, the auction itself, then the whole incident, and then you...I'm drained."

"You put me in that long list as if I'm also–"

She quickly places her finger on my lips to silence me. "No, no. You've been the best thing that's happened in forever. No one has ever stood up for me. There was this one time where I thought a guy would...well, obviously he didn't. So, for you to stand up for me against my dad, saving Izzy and allowing me a chance to get away from where I've always been? I never had a chance or opportunity, and believe me when I say I've wanted to get away many times. But you can't really plan when you have no money and no place to go. So, I can't start to explain how much it all means to me."

"What was the one time a guy didn't and should have?" I question, my curiosity might be drawn but anger is scratching my brain to know why a man wouldn't step up.

Her eyes stay on Izzy when she says, "A few years ago my father walked into the stables and caught me and a guy getting dressed. My father took one glance at me and knew I just had sex. Let's just say I expected Ted to stand up for me when my father started to give me hell, but instead he left."

She doesn't say anything else and I hate filling in the blanks so I have to know, "Did your father hit you?"

A deep sigh flows over her lips along with the whispered words, "Hit, kicked, pushed, ordered me around, and if I wasn't within reach, he would find something to throw at me. I've learned to be compliant all my life but as a teenager I did act up from time to time until it was beaten out of me. What other choice did I have?"

The distant stare isn't a look I want to see. I experienced one incident between her and her father, heard a few words spoken about her past and I'm torn between wanting to know everything for some sweet revenge, and letting go so she can move on. Though, I should leave the past in the past and make damn sure this woman will only know pleasure and positive experiences from here on out.

Knowing more talking will cause her pain with the hurtful reminders, I choose the most sensible option. "Come on, let's get you that shower."

I snatch the bag from the floor and hold out my hand. She laces her fingers with mine and I take the short walk to my cabin. It's small but cozy and holds everything I need. Unlocking the door, I usher her inside and place the bag on the couch.

"Are you a movie fan?" Raney's eyes trail over the old western movie posters I have hanging on the walls of the living room.

"I ordered them online, better than empty walls or posters of naked women." I shoot her a grin and she rolls her eyes. "But, yes. I enjoy watching classics."

I point at a rack filled with old movies and she strolls over to let her fingers slide over the titles. During the ride here we talked for hours and I know she's not completely oblivious to everything going on in the world, though there are some things clearly kept from her.

"Feel free to watch some TV when you're done with your shower. I have to head over to the clubhouse and have a little chat with my president. We sold some horses at the auction and I'm sure Oak brought him up to speed, but I also have to check in."

"Sure, no worries. And I would like to watch a movie with you. I haven't watched one in years. My mother would allow me to see a movie when I was younger but you know how it is with work… up at the crack of dawn and when every task is done, you're drained. Besides, I wasn't allowed in the house after the Ted incident."

Her eyes go to the floor again and the words she said earlier hit me full force again.

"You weren't allowed in the fucking house?" I grunt in anger.

She starts to wring her fucking hands as she gives a faint shake of her head. Yeah. I need to take a breather or I'm going to plant my fist into a wall. I close the distance between us and lift her gorgeous face by placing my finger underneath her chin.

"You left all of it behind when you got into my truck, you hear me? From now on you keep that beautiful head high. This is your home now where I'll take care of you and where you're free to do shit you like to do. No more sleeping in stables or being deprived of basic necessities. And I'll make damn sure you'll have days off to watch a fucking movie or go with the other old ladies to have your hair or nails done or some of the shit women do. Pedicures. Yeah, you're gonna paint your toenails and shit."

Her cheeks heat. "I've never had a pedicure let alone painted my toenails."

"I'm going to rat you out to the old ladies," I murmur right before I give her a slow and sensual kiss.

She needs tenderness and the time needed to

adopt to the changes in her life. I allow the both of us to enjoy our kiss for a few more heartbeats before pulling away.

"Time to show you the bathroom and give you some privacy. I won't be long but take your time. I'll make you some food when I'm back, okay?"

"Sounds like a dream," she shyly says.

"Woman," I growl. "You are the fucking dream."

My mouth covers hers in a rough kiss and it takes every inch of strength to pull away.

"Bathroom is over there. Towels and shit too. Fresh clothes in the bag. I'm sure you'll manage. I have to go now or I won't stop kissing you and most definitely want more but it's not going to happen."

Again, her head falls and the anger inside me makes me snap, "I told you to keep your head high." The words are out before my mind catches up with the realization why she dropped her head.

Releasing a deep sigh, I tell her, "You and I are

happening, Raney. If you don't want there to be anything between us just tell me now and I'll bunk with one of my brothers and give you the space you need. But if you do want there to be an us...we will take it slow. You have been through a lot from the shattered parts I've heard you mention. And I don't want you to feel obligated or do shit with me as a damn thank you. Understood?"

"I want there to be an us. And not just because I'm thankful." There's a truckload of determination in her voice and it's stroking my ego for sure.

"Thank fuck." I chuckle and let my fingertips trail over her jaw. "Go shower and relax."

"Will do." The two words tumble from her lips and I turn to head for the door because if I don't, I'll end up kissing her again.

The walk over to the clubhouse is way too short for me to process my rambling thoughts. This morning I didn't have a woman or so much as the need to have a damn relationship yet now? I want to tie Raney to my bed and keep her there each day to the next.

I've seen men fall for the right woman. It happened to my president, my VP, and a handful of my brothers. They all gave their heart to a woman so it shouldn't come as such a surprise. And it feels right between me and Raney but things about her background are unsettling to say the least.

Stepping inside the large room I notice a few of my brothers sitting at the bar enjoying a beer. Decker strolls out of the office and is holding some papers. He comes to a stop when he sees me and points at church.

"Did they call you?" he questions.

I give a curt shake.

"Come on, Oak filled us in and I called a friend of mine to do a quick check."

Fuck. My blood pressure spikes at the thought of what the results of that check is. Decker used to be FBI and still has those connections. We head into church where my president, Weston, is sitting in his chair with Roper, my VP, right next to him. Oak and Colt are sitting at the table with them along with Spiro.

"Did you get her settled?" my prez questions. "Oak filled us in to make sure we know what we're dealing with and I asked Decker to run a check."

I take a seat across from Oak and lift my chin. "Thanks brother." Oak nods and I direct my attention to Weston. "Everything about this makes me fucking furious. Some of the things she shared about her past? Watching her reaction to some of the shit and what Oak and I witnessed?" I swallow my anger down and shake my head.

Decker takes a seat next to me and pats my back. "Take a few breaths, brother. Because it's going to get a lot worse."

Roper rubs his hands. "Let's hear it."

"Itching to handle something other than your day job or changing diapers?" Weston raises his eyebrow.

"Shut up, you've been elbow deep in diapers too and it's been awhile since we faced some danger. And I just heard our old ladies gush about the new face Garrett brought. Are you going to tell your old lady there's nothing to worry about? Or will you tell her all the fleshy details they want to know because they'll drag them out of us one way or another?"

"I don't want anyone else to know," I snap and glare at each and every one of my brothers. "She's embarrassed enough as it is. Fucking uncomfortable and hasn't slept in a damn bed for fuck knows how long. Hell, she doesn't even know how to read and her fucking father is to blame for everything."

Silence fills the room.

Eventually it's Weston who places his forearms on the table and pierces me with a hard look. "My old lady asked me to make sure Raney felt at home here. You have nothing to worry about when it comes to her being embarrassed or uncomfortable. If anything, I think it's better if everyone is aware of some delicate things so she won't be embarrassed. You're barking up the wrong tree here,

Garrett, and you know it. It's the anger talking, so rein that shit in and let Decker tell us what he found out so we can make arrangements if necessary."

"Sorry, Prez," I grumble.

"I hate to disappoint you guys," Decker starts. "But I've got nothing about Raney."

"Nothing?" Spiro whistles low. "Let me guess, it makes this shit more fucked-up."

"Seems like it." Decker places papers in front of him. "But there's nothing about Raney. She simply doesn't exist. No birth certificate, no social security number, no record whatsoever of her being born or her mother being pregnant. Now her father on the other hand, he does have a record. Fraud, theft, assault, and even murder charges. The murder charges were dropped due to lack of evidence and the body missing for that matter."

Roper releases a string of curses. "Do we have all the details on this guy?"

"Not yet. Nick…well, he's gonna put it on

record so the FBI is going to dig a little deeper. He only gave me a quick rundown but will get back to me as soon as he knows more."

Weston nods at Decker's words. "Church in the morning when you have all the details. And Garrett?"

"Yeah, Prez," I grunt.

"Maybe it would be best to have Raney join us tomorrow morning. She can fill in the blanks. And don't start about her being uncomfortable or embarrassed, she needs to know she has a voice here, okay? From what Oak has told us she...how shall I put it?"

"Has been suppressed all her life? Born to be a slave and work at her father's ranch? No choice, no education, no humanity or equal rights, no fucking nothing? Yeah...she needs to hear and listen to her own voice when she has a say in all of it," I easily finish for him.

Slaps on the table ring out in support while my brothers grunt their agreement. We talk for a few more minutes until there's nothing left to discuss. Time to head back to my cabin and settle in for the night. I have no clue if I'm going to be able to sleep because it's going to be a long damn day tomorrow for sure.

CHAPTER 04

RANEY

"What in the hell are you doing?" a voice barks from behind me.

I drop the cloth I was holding and place my hands over my racing heart.

Gasping for my next breath I tell Garrett, "You scared the crap out of me."

"Good. Now tell me why you're scrubbing my kitchen floor instead of relaxing. Did you even take a fucking shower?"

I scramble off the floor and shake my head.

There's only silence greeting me and I dare to risk a glance in his direction. Shit. He's pissed. I glance down at the floor I was cleaning and think of what to do or say but come up empty.

Whenever my father was pissed or needed someone to blame, I would just stand still and let it wash over me. I guess in this situation I'm opting for the same thing and let my mind wander to Izzy while I wait for him to rain down his wrath. One breath after another flows in and out until I see his boots appear in my vision.

"Eyes, Raney. Give 'em to me." How can his voice carry softness while it held anger a moment ago?

Slowly I meet his gaze and stare at his face which is filled with kindness.

"Care to explain why you're on your knees working when you mentioned you were drained and were going to take a shower and relax?"

"I'm not sure how to explain it, other than the fact that work has always cleared my mind, and my body for that matter. Everything is messy inside my head and then you and your kisses and I couldn't stop thinking, and I saw the muddy prints on your kitchen floor and–" I catch my bottom lip between my teeth to stop my ramblings and cut off my brain before I make more a fool of myself than I already did.

He surprises me by sliding his arm around my waist and pulling me against his body. I can feel him inhale deep and release his breath over the top of my head.

"It's going to be hard as hell to give you your damn life back," he murmurs. "You're falling back on routine. It's work for others while it soothes your restlessness. And the crazy part is…you don't even know it's fucked-up. Just like how you mentioned it's okay if you needed to sleep in the damn stables with Izzy." He pulls back and cups my face to connect our eyes. "No matter the effort, how uncomfortable, awkward, hard, or unthinkable… we're going to make it work. The most important angle in all of this is your happiness. And to be honest, happiness is different for everyone, so who am I to judge if cleaning the floors is what you need to soothe your brain. For me it would be either go for a ride, bike or horse, or put my feet up and watch a movie for the hundredth time."

"I have to keep my hands busy. If I'm with Izzy after the work is done for the day, she lies down and I'll pet her. Most times I also create braided rope halters, lead ropes, and reins. I like braiding rope."

A grin spreads his face. "Braiding rope, huh? I think that could be considered a good hobby."

This might not be a good time to mention my father pressured me to make a few a week and some on demand because he sells them. His finger gently slides across my forehead and in between my eyes.

"Why the lines of worry?" he murmurs.

"I do enjoy making those but it can also be considered work because my father sold them."

"All you ever did was work and earn money for someone else. Yet you have no social security number, no birth certificate, no bed, no money, no clothes, no nothing…even the horse he agreed for you to have after the hard work you did, turned out to be thin air. Fuck." He steps away and releases another string of curses.

I have no clue how to answer or if I even should. My eyes travel to the cloth and how it left a watery stain around it. I'm about to reach for it when my head is being gently cupped and I'm staring into Garrett's soft and gentle eyes again.

"No cleaning for you. You're going to take a shower while I calm down and clean up here. I'm not angry at you. All my anger is rising because of the situation you were in but we're handling it, okay?"

"Okay," I whisper and keep my gaze on his lips.

They curl into a smile and move when he gives me the words, "We're not going to handle it by kissing because I might not be able to resist you when I'm feeling this pumped up. Go on, sugar, enjoy your shower and I'll fix us something to eat."

He spins me around and smacks my ass before pushing me into the direction of the bathroom. I can feel a smile spread my face and stroll into the bathroom, flipping the lights once I'm inside.

This cabin might be tiny but every inch is used to its full extent. The bathroom not only has a large shower but also a bathtub and a sink with a towel rack and a small cabinet. A pile of blue, rolled up, fluffy towels sits on top. I lock the door and strip my clothes before stepping into the shower stall and brace for the cold water.

Grabbing some of the bodywash in my hand I start to quickly wash but am happily surprised by the warmth of the water. I hardly ever have a warm shower. My mother always told me they have bad pipes when I was allowed to take a shower.

But this? I have to adjust the water a bit because it's too hot and it's ahh-mazing. I don't have to hurry and instead I take my time to soap up my body, realizing I'm covering myself with Garrett's scent. I take the shampoo bottle and take a whiff. I keep smiling while I wash my hair.

I suddenly realize Garrett might want to have a shower too and I'm stealing all his hot water. Quickly finishing up, I turn off the shower and grab one of the fluffy looking towels. Heaven. Sweet smelling fluffiness like sunshine being wrapped in the softness of bright blue clouds. I never thought a towel could be this soft.

I rub my body dry and make sure to get most of the water out of my hair and it's then I realize I didn't bring the bag with the clothes Garrett's friends brought me. I wrap the towel around my body and slightly open the door.

"Garrett?"

He steps out of the kitchen with half of his body. "Yeah?"

"Can you please hand me the bag? I forgot to take it with me."

Garrett strolls over to where the bag is and snatches it up. He closes the distance between us and hands it over. His eyes never leave mine and he doesn't so much as steal a glimpse of my body, even if it's mostly covered by the towel.

"Thank you."

He shoots me a wink and spins around, letting the words, "Hope you like spaghetti or else it's just a sandwich," over his shoulder as he disappears into the kitchen.

I close the door and squat down to open the bag and check what's inside. I can't believe my eyes when I pull one piece of clothing after the other from it and they all look new. There are even tags on the panties and sports bra. Most of the clothes are too big but I'm absolutely thankful to receive these gifts; it's more than anyone has ever given me.

Except for what Garrett gave me; a chance, an option, a future. I remove the tags off the clothes and pull on a fresh pair of clothes. I'm drowning a bit in the leggings and the shirt falls mid-thigh but at least it's clean and new.

I follow the mouthwatering scent of spaghetti and stumble onto Garrett who has his back to me. A very naked back with a large tattoo of a horse. The very sexy man is only wearing his jeans and like me he's walking barefoot and somehow it makes him more attractive.

"Have a seat," he says without turning.

I now notice he's set the table for two and I slide into the chair facing him. Garrett carries a large pan over to the table and puts it down between our plates.

"I hope you're hungry." I don't have time to give him words in return when he starts to fill my plate.

He serves himself and takes the seat across from me. I watch how he snatches up his fork and shoves it in the noodles, twirling to roll them and ultimately bring the bundle into his mouth. I grab the fork and mimic his moves.

My mother taught me how to cook when I was growing up. Some things I learned the hard way and I have the burns on my hands and arms to prove it, but I'm mostly good at it and enjoy baking as well. Though most times I wasn't allowed to eat what I made, but that's beside the point. Though the food hitting my tongue is delicious.

"This is really good," I groan and quickly fill my mouth with another load.

"There's enough to feed an army so feel free to eat as much as you like."

"That's a first," I mutter between shoveling another forkful into my mouth.

"My house is yours, my food, my bed, anything you need. And when you're finished, we'll order some stuff online."

The fork freezes on its way to my mouth. "You don't have to do that: your friends gave me enough."

Garrett gives a sharp shake of his head. "You work for me, remember? I need you to wear proper clothing, as your employer I'm responsible."

I keep staring at him and blink a few times. "Are you serious?"

He leans back and crosses his arms in front of his chest. "Employees and employers each have responsibilities, rules, and obligations. The whole world thrives on them for that matter. And I hate to say it but when I went to the clubhouse to meet with my president, Oak already debriefed all of them about what happened at the auction. Decker, one of my brothers who used to be FBI, did a background check. He found out you don't even exist."

I place the fork down, suddenly I'm not that hungry anymore. "I...I don't exist? What do you mean?"

"When someone is pregnant, they have health checks and shit and when the baby is born you file for a birth certificate. You get a number from the government...you need it for a lot of stuff like getting jobs, it identifies you. From what Decker found out there is no record of you. No record of your mother being pregnant, nothing. There is no Raney Bolcord."

"But why? Why would they? I don't understand."

"I should have waited to mention it to you until after you've eaten." Garrett glances at the spaghetti, his gaze softens when his eyes land on mine. "My guess is as good as yours but with the glimpse of your life I've gotten, I'd say he created a free dedicated worker to earn money on his ranch."

I mindlessly nod and pick up my fork. All I've ever known was work. The braiding rope halters was something I saw in a horse magazine one of my father's men gave me. It had step by step pictures, making it easy for me to learn the basics. Most of the other stuff I know I was told by either my parents or the men who worked for my father.

And it was not like they chained me up, I sometimes went with my mother to the store to carry the groceries. I'm not a complete idiot. I also went with my father to sell horses and other stuff;

working at the ranch and around the house is all I've ever known. But my father did tell me once or twice how I would never get anywhere.

Mostly he threw those words at me when I felt rebellious and wanted to see the world and live on my own. Okay, that was a one-time thing right after he ran off Ted. But I now understand what Garrett is saying. My parents put me on this earth for one reason; to use me. Deep down, I've known. Deep down, I knew there wasn't a way out. Not until I met Garrett.

But it also raises the question, "Now what?"

He points at the food in front of me. "Now you eat. Catch your breath, take your time to build something for you while you let us help you. You're not alone, okay?"

I grab my fork and poke at the food.

Garrett's big, tattooed hand covers mine. "It's a lot to take in and with everything that happened today I just want you to know everything might be all fucked-up, but it's also a turning point. One day you're going to look back and remind your-self of the long road you came from compared to the fruitful life you built for yourself."

"Fruitful." I snicker and shove some spaghetti into my mouth, completely oblivious to the taste.

"Bad choice of words, maybe. Just know we're all here for you. Take it one day at a time and to-morrow is a day you'll spend with Izzy. No work, no obligations. And that reminds me, did you start to break her in yet?"

A smile spreads my face at the reminder of Izzy. "I haven't yet but she's used to a bridle and to a saddle. I don't think she needs much work."

"Let me know when and how and we'll make a plan together."

A flock of butterflies assault my stomach and a happy smile spreads my face. "I would like that very much."

"Deal, now eat." He grins and points his fork my way.

My appetite returns and I even grab seconds.

With a full belly we wash the dishes and clean up after ourselves. After another discussion about the sleeping arrangements, we settle on sharing the bed.

It's big enough for the both of us and it's silly for him to give up his bed and sleep on the couch. We're both adults and besides, I might be drained but I'm not used to sleeping in a bed. I'm used to sleeping in the stable with my eyes on Izzy.

And I miss her. It's the middle of the night, darkness surrounds me while Garrett is in a deep sleep beside me. My eyes are burning and it's impossible to sleep. I've been tossing and turning and I'm afraid to wake up Garrett. Sliding out of bed, I tiptoe down the hall and out of the house.

I'm almost at the stables when I hear, "Mind telling me where you're sneaking off to?" rumble through the darkness.

A scream rips from my throat and when the man steps closer, allowing the moon to shine a faint light on his features, I instantly recognize him.

"Oak. You scared the crap out of me."

He doesn't so much as twitch and is still looking at me expectantly.

"I can't sleep. I don't want to wake Garrett. Would it be okay if I sleep with Izzy?"

His eyebrows shoot up. "Sleep with Izzy? As in sleeping with a horse in the stable?"

My cheeks heat and I wring my hands as I whisper, "I haven't slept in a bed in years. I can't sleep."

"For fuck's sake," Oak grumbles underneath his breath. "Come on."

I follow him into the stables and feel some of the restlessness slip away when I see Izzy. Oak opens the door for me and I step inside to let my fingers slide over her coat.

"Here you go. And you better not run off with Garrett's property, ya hear? Look."

My gaze snaps to his.

He's pointing at black orbs on the ceiling.

"Every inch of this ranch has eyes on everything at all times, understood?"

Feeling embarrassed by his suggestion I would steal from Garrett and run off with Izzy to go... where? Back to my parents because life was awesome? The things I've experienced today were some of the best things I had in years. The food in my belly for one, not to mention my horse is still with me and well taken care of.

All of it makes me snap, "I wouldn't betray the first good thing that entered my life. I don't expect you to understand but I will see it for what it is and thank you for standing up for your friend. I would be thankful to call him or you that one day too. Though I like to think he already is my friend for the way he was the first person who stood up for me."

Oak doesn't say anything in return and merely shakes his head and strolls away. I take a deep breath and close the stable, taking a seat in the corner in the warm bedding and lean my head against the door. My eyes fall shut and with each breath I regain calmness with the scent of Izzy as I drift off to sleep.

CHAPTER 05

One week later

GARRETT

Oak opens the stable for me and I step inside. Izzy doesn't so much as twitch when I scoop Raney up who once again slipped out of the bed and into the stables. It was exactly one week ago when Oak woke me up to tell me where Raney was. I have been dragging her back to bed every single night since.

At least she's been waking up in bed every morning, but falling asleep in it plagues her mind. During the day she's the complete opposite.

Maybe because all she knows is working at a ranch, but she falls right into the routine of helping and working. With the horses as well as the other livestock, along with every chore around the ranch.

Hell, she helped me rebuild part of a fence as if I had one of my brothers assist me. And when I gave her different kinds of rope a few days ago, she braided a stunning rope halter for Izzy. One Alfie, along with many other brothers, wanted and have asked her to make one for each of them in return for money.

I carefully place her on the mattress and she turns to curl into herself. Thankfully she keeps sleeping as I stare down upon her. Not only does she fit in here on the ranch, she's also been working very hard to take steps in learning how to read.

Six days ago, I had a meeting with my brothers in church. We discussed her whole situation. They wanted her to join us but I decided to keep her out of it. In my opinion she didn't need the added stress of everyone discussing her life and the details Decker found out.

The first night with her taught me that; she had enough demons clawing at her brain. What she needs is a clean break. It's the reason I burned the note she thought was a contract, making sure she wouldn't ever be able to read it. I don't want her to read or hear things that can hurt her.

And I knew I made the right choice when Spiro questioned if Raney wasn't scamming me. Knowingly being in on the stuff her father was a part of where sometimes he would sell horses and later come back to steal them along with a few others, forging papers to sell them again. I lunged for Spiro's throat and it's a good thing Oak held me back because I was ready to kill a brother over this woman. That's how deep she's already managed to crawl underneath my skin.

I slide underneath the covers and pull her against me. She snuggles closer and puts her head on my chest. It pains me to know how she seeks me out in her sleep and is comfortable to snuggle close and yet the restlessness and lack of inner trust draws her to the routine of falling asleep in the stable.

But then I think about how well she's progressing with learning letters and reading. After the meeting I had with my brothers almost a week ago some of the old ladies came to me and asked to help Raney settle in. I took my brothers' advice to save her from embarrassment and shame and spilled some details, one of those being her lack of reading skills.

They jumped right in and bought her a stack of flashcards with letters and words on one side and illustrations on the back to help her. Shit kids use to learn and to be honest? I didn't even think about doing this or have any idea where to start. The old ladies took over, and in a way, it made her also adapt into their group as well.

A few days ago, I asked if she needed my help with the cards, pulling random ones and letting her tell me what letter or word. Her cheeks turned red and I had no clue why. Until she quickly grabbed a stack of cards with words on them and they all tumbled onto the floor.

Seems Kadence made an added stack of cards to teach her dirty words. I got a good laugh out of that and couldn't help but tease her. She ended up slapping my chest and ordered me to pick up the cards since it was my fault they ended up on the floor. I did and couldn't help but hold up each card to make her read it out loud for me.

What has also been helping is the phone I bought her. After explaining how it worked, we started texting and the smile on her face was price-less when she read my first text out loud. One sim-ple "Hi," never held so much meaning. And it was the same when she texted me back the same word.

Progress takes time and not every angle has the same speed. But for now, I'm damn proud of my woman and I hope she feels and knows how far she's already come. My woman. I relish in the way this statement sounds inside my head and realize she's actually rooted deeper underneath my skin than I originally thought. I kiss the top of her sleeping head and release a deep breath, content to finally fall asleep with my woman in my arms and safely in my bed.

The sun shining through the curtains wakes me up way too early on my day off and I realize my arms are empty. A groan ripples through me and I slant my arm over my eyes. The softest of laughter enters my ears and I take a squinted peek from underneath my arm. Raney is sitting crossed-legged, staring at me with a smile on her face.

"What's so funny?" I question and close my eyes in an effort to catch some more sleep, though I know it's futile.

"You," Raney quips and I automatically smile and let my arm drop from my face when I hear her blurt, "You make me happy."

Her face turns red and her eyes go wide but I love her honesty and the way she always catches herself after blurting out her thoughts. The redness tinging her cheeks always shows her innocence. She might think it's either shame or embarrassment but I think it's endearing.

I jolt up and cup the side of her face, letting my thumb trail over her heated cheek. "Good," I murmur. "Because you make me damn happy too."

I decide to pop a question at her to create a distraction because her eyes still hold slight panic due to the thoughts and feelings she just shared.

"Are you ready for today?"

The smile sliding over her face is blinding.

Yes," she says with determination. "We have another hour before we're meeting the others. We're going on your bike, right?"

"Yeah." I feather my lips softly against hers.

These last few days we've only stolen some kisses here and there. I was determined to give her space to get on her feet but it's been difficult not to strip her naked, drag her against my body and have my wicked way with her. But I guess with our admittance–the both of us being happy with one another–it's time to take the next step.

The next step being sex. I make a mental note to buy some condoms since we're headed into town with my prez and VP–along with their old ladies–later today. It's why I asked if she was ready for today.

"Let's get this day started with some coffee. I'm sure I'll need a cup or three to wake up. Damn it feels as if I skipped sleep completely," I grumble and swing my legs off the bed.

"I'm sorry." Her soft voice flows through the air and I spin around to face her.

"What for?" I reach for my jeans and pull them over my boxers.

I take a few steps in the direction of the bathroom when she says, "For sleeping in the stable again."

Her eyes are fixed on her hands while she's plucking at the bedsheet.

Stepping closer to the bed, I lean in and lift

her chin with one finger to make sure she sees the truth in my eyes when I tell her, "Some things require a process. Old habits can also take longer to break, even more when feelings are involved and it's been a routine for many years. I don't care if I have to keep dragging you back to this bed, spread horse bedding all over our bed, or bring Izzy into our bedroom for that matter. One day you will allow yourself to fall asleep in our bed. And that day will be fucking perfect because it will mean I will get to hold you while we fall asleep together."

Her hands are gripping my head the next instant and she merges her lips with mine. Her tongue slides past my lips and I greedily take what she gives. Our kiss turns feverish when I sneak my arm around her waist to pull her body flush against mine. Fucking heaven.

She's still the one in control with her hands cupping my head and I relish in her boldness to take what she wants. My dick is hard and luckily safely locked behind the teeth of my zipper. It's a good thing otherwise I'd rip off her pants and bury myself deep.

Condoms. My job for the day is to buy condoms and a large damn box to make sure we have enough for the foreseeable future. Raney breaks the kiss and buries her head into the crook of my neck.

"You really, *really* make me happy, Garrett." Her words are a soft whisper against my skin.

A groan rips from the back of my throat. "Wait till we have a box of condoms, we'll add a few more reallys in front of the 'make me happy' statement."

She giggles against my neck and I give her a tight hug before letting go and tell her, "I'm gonna make some coffee. I'm sure the women will be here soon."

"We agreed to meet in the clubhouse fifteen minutes before we leave. Harlene and Cassidy had to go to the clinic to handle a few things, we couldn't meet up sooner or they would have been here already." Her eyes slide to the bed and she takes a step closer to me. "We could…kiss some more…and more."

"Good to know." I shoot her an apologetic smile. "But I don't have any condoms, and believe me when I say we're going to rectify that as soon as we head into town."

"Good to know," she echoes.

The longing and lust in her eyes is making my dick harder. I have to clear my throat and adjust myself, trying like hell to think about anything other than burying myself deep inside her sweet pussy. Yeah. Not helping.

"Coffee," I croak. "We need coffee."

"Good thing we're both off today and only have a few hours planned in town for some shopping. That leaves the rest of the day to spend together."

I have to blink a few times but my heart fucking jumps about the fact she's straightforward and wants this as much as me, that's for damn sure.

"We might need more than the rest of the day,"

I murmur and step closer.

She tips her head back to look into my eyes while her arms slide around my waist.

Her voice is a mere whisper but it rings loud inside my ears when she says, "Maybe tonight I'll be too sated to leave your bed."

"Now there's something to dream about." I brush my nose gently against hers, giving her the words, "We're saving the best for later. Come on. Coffee, before I say the hell with it and knock you up so you won't ever leave me."

Her eyes go wide and she jumps away from me. "We can't. I never even gave it one single thought about having children, becoming a mom, a parent. I don't even know what parents should be like since mine were clearly twisted. It's...no. I'm–"

I know it's a shitty situation but I can't help it when a slight chuckle rips from me and I point a finger in her direction. "Why do you think I'm still wearing pants pressing for the both of us getting coffee? We have all the time in the world, sugar.

No rush, no pressure, no kids for now, just us."

She closes the distance between us and I know we're going to end up tangled in a hot kiss that's going to make my dick un-fucking-breakable.

"Coffee," I croak once more.

Her eyes lower to my crotch and she swallows hard. She wets her damn lips before biting down on her bottom one. If she keeps this up I'll blow my load inside my pants; that's how much I crave her.

I spin on my heels and head into the bathroom to freshen up, locking the door behind me to be sure I have time to cool down. When I've handled my business and stroll back into the bedroom, I find it empty.

Pulling on my boots, a shirt along with my cut, I go in search of Raney and find her in the kitchen. She holds out a cup filled with steamy black goodness. The corner of her mouth twitches and it's a look I love on her; relaxed and happy.

"Have you made a list of the things you'd like

to buy?" I question as I take a seat at the kitchen table.

She joins me and pulls a piece of paper from her jeans pocket and hands it over. Instead of words she drew the items she needs. As agreed I've kept my end of the deal and gave her cash for the first week she worked for me. I have talked her salary through with Weston, not wanting to cut her short or make her uncomfortable if I gave her more than necessary.

The look she gave me yesterday showed me she wasn't expecting that much money while it was still at a normal rate. Raney might have been kept underneath her father's thumb but she's damn smart. It shows in all the things she does and how quick of a learner she is.

And the money I gave her is safely kept in a jar in our bedroom while she took out a small cut she's going to spend. And the smart part? She's buying necessities to braid halters and ropes she received orders for since everyone on this ranch loves her creations.

Passion, relaxation, whatever; braiding is another way for her to create an income. She's doing all of this to buy Izzy back, the way I promised her. But to be honest? The horse has a value beyond recognition and she won't be able to afford Izzy because Raney is tied to her and I'm not going to give that woman up; she's mine.

The thought of her being my woman settles my raging heart and the pounding need rushing through my veins. We just discussed future stuff like kids and throwing out feelings and solidifying there actually is an us.

This leaves me one more thing to do today; voice my claim to my prez to officially make Raney my old lady.

CHAPTER 06

RANEY

I have my own money in my pocket and my arms wrapped around the hottest man alive. Not to mention, we're on our way to buy condoms because there's an us. This is a moment I will remember and treasure for a long time.

Any moment spent with Garrett is one to remember. From the day I met him I've only experienced good moments. There's just one hard part in all of this and that's falling asleep. I'm absolutely exhausted but the restlessness in my bones doesn't allow me to fall asleep in the bed next to Garrett.

I do wake up in the bed next to him and it warms my heart to know he cares enough to get up and drag my sleeping body back into bed with him. I know it's not the sleeping part I have issues with but I guess I'm afraid to fall asleep and realize my life was a dream…not wanting the day to end and wake up in the hell I have been living in. Or whatever the reason for me not being able to fall asleep in a bed like a normal person.

Hopefully one day. It warms my heart how he mentioned he'd even cover our mattress with horse bedding or drag Izzy into our bedroom if it would help. He really has all the patience, strength, and ability to help. *He cares*. And in return I adore him. Every day I fall a little more for this man and it's both scary and amazing all in one go.

And I absolutely love this bike ride. Garrett controls his machine flawlessly while I hold on as I'm plastered against his strong back.

He skillfully guides the bike around the corner and comes to a stop right next to Weston's bike. Harlene dismounts and gives me a smile.

Another thing I enjoy about living with Garrett; I now have a whole group of friends. And it's not about them being nice because Garrett told them to; their intentions are real. I've noticed it the first few days when they offered to help me with learning how to read.

The laughs and spending time without so much as a complaint and wanting to meet up again and again…everything shows these people like me for who I am. I return the smile and wait for the bike to stop roaring. The vibrations die and Garrett pats my thigh, indicating I can get off.

My legs are wobbly but I've very much enjoyed the ride and can't wait to get back on again. But first we have some shopping to do. My cheeks heat at the reminder of Garrett mentioning we need a few large boxes of condoms so we won't run out any time soon.

I've only had sex twice, and neither time was worth mentioning, but I get the feeling it will be very different with Garrett. For one because I'm physically drawn to him and have developed feelings, adding to the need to be with him; to feel more connected. But mostly due to our kisses rising more excitement and heat through my whole body than I've ever experienced.

Garrett places his hand on the small of my back and guides me toward Weston, Roper, Harlene, and Cassidy. We all head into the hardware store where I pick up the items I jotted down to make different braided halters.

The guys have to swing by the butcher next for the meat order they placed. We're having a barbeque on Friday and most of the shopping will be done tomorrow morning but the girls wanted to marinate and prepare the meat and that's why we're picking it up today.

Weston places a kiss on Harlene's lips. "Call if something is up. We'll meet you guys in front of the store, okay?"

Garrett leans in next to my ear. "I'll go into the store when we're done at the butcher so I can grab a few boxes of condoms."

My cheeks heat and I bury my fist into his leather cut to keep him close and cover up my red cheeks. The bastard chuckles and places a kiss on the top of my head.

"No worries, I'll get enough to keep us going for–" His sentence ends in a grunt when I plant my fist in his gut.

"Enough," I grumble.

Laughter falls from his lips and he pulls me close to give me a kiss, one where everything around us falls away until a few throats clear behind us.

Garrett breaks the kiss and tells me, "Stay with the other old ladies. You can always call if something is up."

"I know, no worries," I promise him and the girls drag me toward the shop while the guys head for the butcher.

I have a backpack for the stuff I already bought so my hands are free to do some more shopping. Taking a shower has now become a routine and using Garrett's bodywash is nice but getting my own scent would be amazing.

It's the first task the girls take very seriously and I think they've shoved eight different bottles underneath my nose before I can so much as take one whiff. And they all smell amazing. I still haven't made a decision when Kadence and Harlene check out the other products in the next aisle.

I finally find a bodywash I like. It's a vanilla and raspberry scent and I'm grabbing similar shampoo when I hear my name being hissed from an aisle behind me. A chill runs up my spine when recognition sets in.

Holding the shampoo and bodywash against my chest I spin around and face my father. He's ducked behind the different products on the shelves and his eyes are set over my shoulder. A quick glance lets me know he's watching Harlene and Cassidy.

"Time to come home, Raney," my father hisses underneath his breath. "Playtime is over."

Fear grips me and I refuse to let my father ruin things for me. For the first time in my life, I feel like I belong and every day is filled with joy and happiness. I'm not giving up my life with Garrett; he reminds me every day I have a choice to live life my own way without taking orders from anyone.

I take a step closer and hiss back, "There is no playtime, I have my own life now."

His eyes go hard and he releases a sinister laugh. "Stupid girl. You have no life. You only have what I give you. And if you think that man you're fucking gives a shit about you, you're wrong. He might like to fuck you but you're not the only one he's fucking. He'll grow tired of you and kick you out and you'll have nothing."

"You made me think Izzy was mine and you

sold her. I had nothing when he offered me a chance to start over," I snap.

"That stupid horse was never yours. Your job is to take care of the horses so I can sell them when they're ready. That horse was ready to make me some money and you had others to work with waiting for you, you ungrateful bitch." His eyes focus over my shoulder and he slightly crouches while his voice lowers some more. "Get your ass home. Work needs to be done so stop being selfish by thinking with your cunt. If it's the fucking you want, I'm sure I can get one of the men to do you or maybe you can work that job nights so we can make more money. I'll even give you some too. And that's me being nice. I've been watching you, Raney. I know your every move. I meant what I said: you have no life, only what I give you. And if you stay here? I'll kill every single one of them, one by one and I'm going to start with that guy whose bike you were on, and then I'll kill all those chicks you laugh around with." His chin jerks in

Cassidy and Harlene's direction, making my blood freeze. "And I'll make sure to shoot that horse you pine over. Don't think I won't. Remember Ted? That bastard who kept you from your work? He didn't live for very long after I caught him. Your cowboy biker will follow in his footsteps and end up in the ground as well. I gave you everything, even life itself, you ungrateful bitch, and I'll take it all away. Home. Now."

He turns and rushes out of the store. I'm frozen to the floor while my head is spinning. Ted. The guy he caught me with and who I never saw again. Did my father just insinuate he killed him? How he is going to kill Garrett and every single one of my newfound friends? Kill Izzy? My chest feels like I'm being crushed between two walls and there's no room for me to take my next breath.

"Was that man bothering you?" Harlene stalks toward me while Cassidy runs out of the store, probably to go after him.

"I want to go home," I muse, the things my

father threw at me are still slicing through my brain.

I'm clutching the two items with one arm and shove my free hand into my pocket to reach for my phone. It only takes a few swipes of my thumb to call Garrett.

"We're almost there, sugar." His voice is warm and soothing and I close my eyes to let those words calm me down. "A handful of minutes and we'll be buying those condoms and heading home."

This is what I needed; a distraction to pull me out of the darkness my father threw at me.

"Hey, is everything okay? Is Cassidy there with you? Harlene?" he questions, the words holding concern.

"She's here." I glance at Harlene and she takes the phone from my hands.

"Hey, Garrett, it's me, Harlene. Where are you guys? Okay, we're going to pay for our stuff and meet you outside. Yes. Okay."

She hangs up and gives me my phone back.

"Come on, let's get out of here. The guys will be here within five minutes and then we'll head home."

Cassidy stalks toward us, she's slightly out of breath. "The dude was fast. What did he say to you? Do you know who he was?"

I mindlessly nod as we head for the cashier.

"The guys will be here in a few minutes, we're going to head home," Harlene tells Cassidy.

"The guys are here," Garrett rumbles and pierces me with his gaze. "Are you okay? What happened?"

"There was a creepy guy–"

Harlene starts, but I cut her off. "My father, he was here."

"Fuck." Garrett releases another string of curses and pulls me close.

"I'm okay now," I croak.

He pulls back and glances down at me. "Yeah, you are. Come on, let's get back to the clubhouse."

I stay rooted to the floor while Cassidy and

Harlene walk over to Roper and Weston.

"What's wrong?" Garrett asks.

The concern is vivid in his eyes and it makes my chest squeeze to know how much he cares about me. Such a stark contrast with my father, and I now clearly see the lies he has been telling me. Not to mention how stupid I've been all my life. Why didn't I see how my parents basically chained me to them to work while giving me nothing in return other than a roof above my head and some scarce food to keep up my strength?

"Nothing is wrong," I tell him with determination, fighting the fear so my father won't ruin this thing between Garrett and me. "I would like to pay for these and we need–" I lower my voice and whisper, "Condoms. Let's not let my father ruin everything."

He gives me a smile and cups the side of my face to give me a soft and quick kiss. "Yeah, you're absolutely right."

Garrett takes the bodywash and shampoo from

my hands and adds three boxes of condoms. He pays for them while I try to object and pay myself but the cashier has already put the items in a bag and gives him the change.

We head for the bikes and I should feel worried due to the confrontation with my father and yet Garrett's protective arm around me offers me all the comfort and strength I need to keep my head high.

I don't ever want to go back to where I was. Every day since I arrived at the Iron Hot Blood ranch has been one wrapped with warmth and fun in a relaxed environment. No matter the hard work I also participated in. Somehow none of it was a chore and I did it with a huge smile on my face.

Not to mention, I had Garrett's company through all of it and the knowledge Izzy was well taken care of and I could go to her any time of day. And the hot showers, the food, the friendships, all of it is such a stark contrast to what was once my life. So, I'm going to fight for what I want;

my dream.

The ride back allows me the time to let my brain settle with the decision to leave the past for what it is. My father has told me many lies and the one about Ted must have been one too. He's just angry I'm not doing all the work anymore and he has to do it himself or hire extra people to do it for him.

We arrive at the ranch and I expect Garrett to take me to his cabin but instead he guides us into the clubhouse. Cassidy and Harlene both shoot me comforting smiles as Garrett guides me into the room they call church.

Roper and Weston stroll in behind us and Decker, along with Oak step inside as well before the door falls shut behind them. Garrett pulls out a chair and takes one for himself right next to me. The other men take a seat while the silence in the room is deafening.

I know this is all about me and what just happened. Here I was ready to leave the past in the past and yet I realize it's just running with my head tucked in my ass because there is no escaping your past unless it's resolved.

"Can you please tell us what your father said?" Garrett starts.

His tone might be soft and supportive but the looks I'm getting from all the other men feels like I'm a threat in the room they need to extinguish. And I realize they're right. I am pulling all of them into my past where my father is coming back to haunt me.

I was stupid to think I could live the dream because it felt like it was within my reach with Garrett at my side, but it was foolish. My father won't rest until I'm back and who knows what lengths he'll go through to get me back.

Would he? Am I willing to take the risk and put all of their lives on the line? Because what if there's the slightest chance he did kill Ted and will kill Garrett? I never saw Ted or Ted's father again for that matter. My father has hurt me many times. He would. Sadness and fear hits me hard. If something would happen to Garrett or any of my new friends, I could never live with myself.

"I'm sorry. All of you gave me so much." I stand and turn to Garrett. "Thank you. For everything." My eyes start to burn and my throat clogs up. I have to force out the words I need for him to hear before I start to sob and turn into a mess and can't speak. "I don't want to buy Izzy back because she loves it here and is in good hands with you, I can see this now. I...I have to go. Thanks. All of you, from the bottom of my heart."

Tears are streaming down my face as I dash through the room, swing the door open and head for the exit.

CHAPTER 07

GARRETT

I rush after my woman and manage to grab her by the waist. "Now wait just a goddamned second."

She pushes away from me and with tears streaming down her face she yells, "No. I can't. You have to let me leave. Forget about me, Garrett. There is no other way."

"Fuck that," I growl and snatch her wrist to pull her toward me.

I bend my knees and shove my shoulder into

her belly to hoist her up and carry her–fireman style–back into church. I kick the door shut and slide her down my body. Cupping her face with both hands I keep her eyes locked on mine. Even if she sees me as a blurry mess, she needs to hear what I have to say and know I mean every damn word.

"I won't ever forget about you because you're rooted underneath my goddamned skin. You're mine, Raney. Mine to care for, to protect, to cherish, and mine to damn well claim right here in front of my brothers. Whatever you're facing you're not alone. So, no. You're not leaving, and there's always another way. You don't have a wall behind your back with no way out, but a solid brotherhood who protects no matter what."

The tears keep flowing over her cheeks and are wetting my hands. My heart is near bursting just from the look of gratification mixed with adoration and warmth. She crashes her body against mine and wraps her arms so damn tight around me it's hard to damn well breathe.

"I don't want to lose you," she croaks between sobs.

I rub her back and kiss the top of her head. "You're not getting rid of me this easy, sugar."

She pulls back, face red and wet but she's still breathtakingly gorgeous and all mine. "My father threatened to kill you if I didn't go back. And at first, I thought it was all lies. He's lied so many times…but then he mentioned Ted, and seeing you guys all together…it just hit me…what if there was a slight chance…I can't risk you getting hurt." Her head swings to the right to face my brothers. "Any of you for that matter. You've all been sweet and kind. I can't risk your lives."

"Good, 'cause we're not risking yours either, doll," Decker states. "A friend of mine will be arriving any second. He contacted me today about a few things concerning your father. The day you got here two brothers looked out for you and we took it to the table. We have been trying to get things set for you to help get the paperwork done. My friend, Nick, who is FBI, mentioned your father has been a murder suspect but the charges were dropped due to lack of evidence and a body. But Nick reopened the case this morning. You mentioned your father said something about Ted? Mind explaining what that was about?"

Her eyes return to me and the red on her cheeks deepens. Fucking hell, she's ashamed of the situation she's in and talking about what she mentioned to me isn't helping either; confessing to it with a room full of men.

"You didn't do anything wrong, love," I murmur and raise my voice to let my brothers know, "Her dad caught my woman and Ted after they messed around. Ted didn't stand up for her or face her father. She simply never saw him again."

"He was the son of one of your father's employees, right?" Weston questions and Raney nods in reply.

Roper clears his throat to gain my woman's

attention. "Anything else your father threaten you with?"

She shakes her head a little too quick for my liking.

I put my finger underneath her chin and let our gaze collide. "You can tell us anything. We will never judge you, okay?"

Her eyes go down and I really hate the fact this woman has to feel ashamed on many occasions. We will put all of this behind us as soon as possible so I can make sure she'll never have to suffer discomfort inflicted by her parents.

Her words are a mere whisper but I easily pick up on them. "He mentioned if I was with you for the fucking. He said he could put me to work for that too...make more money and how he would give me some of that."

"Motherfucker," I growl and drag her against my chest.

Curses flow through the air and by the anger written on my brothers' faces I say they easily picked up on her whispered words as well.

"Garrett, take your old lady home. She's your number one priority. And for now, she's on lockdown because we're not taking any chances. We don't want that fucker coming anywhere near her and we have security cams all over the ranch so if he comes here, we have him on tape. As soon as Nick gets here we'll discuss how to ban him from her life for good."

I'm about to thank my prez but Raney beats me to it when her voice soft and small croaks, "Thank you so much. I don't know what else to say but know this means a lot. I...this...so much."

"You're family now, Raney," Weston simply replies. "Let your old man take you home."

Her head bobs as I guide her out the door. She seems a million miles away when we step inside the cabin. There's a knock on the door and I check before opening it but notice Harlene standing on the porch.

"Here." She hands me the bag of stuff we

bought and also Raney's backpack. "I thought she might like these. You know, if she wanted to braid something to relax or shower with her own scent. She took a long time picking the one she loved the most."

"Thanks." I give my president's old lady a smile. "Appreciate it."

"Make sure she knows we're all here for her." She raises her voice and tilts her head to look around me. "You hear me, Raney? We're all here for you and now that you've found us, we won't let you go. You're our friend, friends stick together."

I'm pushed to the side by Raney's body when she launches herself at Harlene to pull her into a hug. With all the tears streaming down her cheeks in church, I would think she doesn't have any left. Yet these seem like happy tears and I have to say, Harlene adds a few of her own as well.

After a few minutes and when most of the tears have dried, Harlene pulls back and rubs Raney's upper arms. "I heard you're Garrett's old lady now."

"News travels fast," I grumble underneath my breath.

Harlene shoots me a smile. "President's old lady, remember? When my friend walks out of the clubhouse looking like she did? You can damn well expect me to ask my man what the hell happened."

"Appreciate you looking after her," I honestly tell her.

Raney slides her arm around my waist and leans against me. "You guys really are something."

I give her a squeeze. "You fit right in since you really are something too, sugar."

"I'll leave you guys to it. Call me or text if you need anything." Harlene waves as she walks back to the clubhouse.

We should go inside but the change from being miles away to leaning against me with a content sigh and slight smile tugging her lips suits me better after the short visit Harlene brought us.

A black SUV comes down the road and I can

feel Raney's body freeze.

I give a comforting kiss on the top of her head. "Relax, I recognize the SUV, it's Nick. Like Weston said, let them handle it. Your job is to relax."

She glances up. "Mind taking a shower with me?"

"A shower? With you?" I'm instantly rock-hard at the thought of being naked and in close proximity of one another.

She gives me a shy smile and her cheeks pinken adorably. "I bought new bodywash and shampoo and I would like to know what it feels like to take a shower with my own stuff. As a couple we could shower together, right? Because you're mine too, you know…since I'm yours."

I let my lips meet hers and slide my tongue inside her mouth to take hers on a sensual dance. One of her arms sneaks up and around my neck as she presses her body closer to mine. I grab her ass and she's as light as a damn feather as I hoist her up.

I walk into the cabin and close the door, flipping the lock to make sure we have enough privacy. I only break the kiss to search for the bag and take it with us as I carry her into the bathroom where I place her down on her feet.

Turning on the water, I take out the shampoo and bodywash before I start to strip away all my clothes. Raney's gaze is on me while she rips off her clothes and lets them fall to the floor. Her eyes might still be puffy but they carry a load of heat.

And where there were different kinds of emotions taking the upper hand back in the clubhouse, right now they're burning with lust, adoration, and a deeper meaning. One I also feel inside my bones and pulses through my body with every squeeze of my heart.

I hold out my hand and she slides her fingers over my palm. Stepping underneath the water, I take her with me and let my hands roam. She grabs the bodywash and squirts a fair amount on her hand.

There's a twinkle of mischief in her eyes when she says, "I've been smelling like you for days, I'd say it's time for you to smell like me."

I hold my hands out. "By all means, I'm yours."

And damn does it feel magnificent to get soaped-up by my woman. There's no trace of stress tugging at her brain, no worries of the world pushing us around; there's only us. Her hand slides down and a groan rips from my throat when her delicate fingers start to fondle my balls.

More fingers join the party and wrap around my hard length. My arms flash forward to brace myself against the tiles, my woman caged in between as I surrender myself to the feelings she draws out deep inside me.

If she feels this good with her mere hands, I'm dying to know what it would be like to bury myself deep inside her pussy. Her movements might be slightly inexperienced but glancing down at her face, eyes intrigued and filled with desire, it's sexy as fuck.

It catches me by surprise when my orgasm hits. Cum shoots out over her hand and her stomach. A fucking straight aim to brand my woman as mine. Her hands fall away when I step closer and cage her between my body and the tiles. A gasp tumbles from her lips, probably due to the cold tiles.

I take advantage to slam my mouth over hers, teeth clashing from the force of uncaged hunger she erupted inside my body. I might have blown my load but I'm nowhere near sated. And it's exactly what this kiss is telling her when my tongue starts to fuck her mouth the way I want to dominate her pussy.

She clings to my body, raises her leg to curl around mine so she can press her pussy against my cock and it's damn near heaven. My mind is triggered by the warning how we need a condom because it's too damn easy to shift my hips and sink balls deep.

A frustrated groan rumbles from my chest and I turn the water off, keeping Raney close as I stalk out of the bathroom and head for the living room to grab the bag. I'm balancing her ass on one hand and with her legs locked around my waist I easily carry her back to the bedroom.

I let her bounce on the bed. I rip the box of condoms open and the things go flying all over the place. Snatching one off the bed I rip open the foil and quickly cover myself. My eyes find my woman.

Waterdrops still sliding off her body, hair plastered against her skin, and eyes wide with desire. Her pussy is glistening in a warm welcome and it draws the need to taste her. Leaning in I do just that but I'm stopped when she's holding my head.

Eyes wide she gasps. "What are you doing?"

A sly smile spreads my face. "Gonna taste my woman. Eat your pussy and suck out an orgasm before I bury my cock inside you over and over again."

"That's not. You can't." She swallows hard. "Really? Kiss me…there?"

I blow a hot breath over her wet flesh and watch how her whole body shivers, and it's not from the fucking cold.

"Yeah, really. This pussy is all mine and judging from your reaction I'd say I'm the first one, and most definitely the last, who will taste you."

Her hands linger for a few more breaths until they fall away. Her eyes stay pinned on me when I lean in and flatten my tongue against her pussy, licking her from ass to clit in one go. She tastes as good as I imagined and I slide my arms underneath her ass to tilt her hips and settle in.

"Oh, gosh. That's...oh. Garrett." My name on a long moan while she releases short gasps in between words is ego stroking to know I'm bringing her pleasure no one else ever gave her.

It doesn't take long for her taste to intensify. A few combined nibbles with my teeth grazing her clit, sucking on her pussy and spearing her with my tongue lights her up like the brightest of stars on a dark night. She screams my name and holds my head in place while grinding herself against my face.

I should give her time to come down from her high but I'm too damn close to blowing my next load into a condom while I haven't even felt her pussy wrapped around me. She's driving me absolutely insane and I relish in it.

Tearing myself lose from her tight grip, I surge up and place the blunt head of my cock against her hot and puffy lips. Balancing on one hand next to her head I watch closely as I start to thrust. Her nails dig into my back, eyes locked on mine, lips parted and the sexy as fuck gasps break my restraint as I throw my hips forward and slam inside.

"Fuuuuuuck," I growl at the ceiling. "So fucking tight and good."

I slowly tip my head down to watch my woman and she gives me a shy smile. Her face is flushed and this time there's no shame or discomfort; only pleasure.

Without a second thought, and drunk on lust

and desire, I spill my real feelings. "Feeling this good when we're connected, it makes me adore you more than life itself."

"If this is our first time, I think we might do better the next time," she replies tartly.

A bark of laughter makes my hips falter but I quickly overtake the pounding I was giving her. I don't think I've ever laughed during sex and this woman manages to bring out every single element into our moment, making it special and unique.

Exactly what her pussy feels like; special and unique. I already came once in the shower and it should allow me to last longer but when I feel her walls start to strangle me, head throwing back to voice my name on a moan as pleasure consumes her…I have no other choice but to follow her into a sea of bliss.

And if it's this intense our first time, it has a load of promise for the future.

CHAPTER 08

RANEY

I watch Garrett's tight, muscled butt head for the bathroom to dispose of the condom. I can't believe this handsome, sexy, strong, muscled, tattooed man is all mine. The fierce way he dragged me back once I told him I couldn't put any of them in danger really stole my heart.

And the way he acted makes me think I won't ever get it back. Not that I'm worried since I'm pretty sure I stole his just now. Sex is ahh-mazing. Mind blowing and orgasm-shattering. I've never experienced pleasure coursing through my veins the way this man took hold of me and worshipped my body.

I simply don't have any other way to put it. And I feel deliciously sore and sated as I watch Garrett stroll back to the bed. He leans in and brushes his fingertips along my cheek so tender and loving, it makes my heart skip with joy.

"I like this look on you," he murmurs and leans in for a kiss.

I eagerly kiss him back but he pulls away with a soft chuckle.

"I don't think your pussy is ready for a second pounding yet, sugar. And I should be sorry for going a bit rough on you but you dragged me into the moment where I could barely breathe unless I chased an orgasm for the both of us."

"I'm not complaining. I'll never complain about something that feels so good." I push myself up and sit on my knees to be on eye level with him since he's still standing beside the bed.

"Good," he gruffly replies. "Wanna do something fun before we go for another round?"

Deciding to live in this magical moment where not only my body but my whole life feels great, I simply hum, "Hmmm. Something more fun than we just did? Count me in."

He gives me a goofy grin. "Nothing beats sex with you."

"That we can agree on," I admit in all honesty.

His head tips back and laughter rips out. I watch how this strong, naked man tightens his muscles while he's completely relaxed.

When he faces me again, he grabs my wrist and pulls me against him. "Don't ever change and don't let anyone tell you how to live your life. You know damn well what you want and enjoy so grab every second like it was yesterday and live for the now."

I slide my arms around him. "I'm already living in the now. It happened when you stepped in my path and guided me into the whole 'too good to be true, dreaming while being wide awake' road of life."

"Our road of life," he murmurs and places a kiss on my lips. "How about we go check on Izzy or go for a ride through the pastures to check on the livestock? We have to stay on the property, though."

I quickly nod and step away to grab some clothes. When I'm fully dressed he takes my hand and we head out through the back.

"What would you like to do? Check on Izzy or go for a ride?" he questions.

"Both," I instantly reply. "We check on Izzy first, saddle up and enjoy the afternoon on horse-back."

There's a large van in front of the stables and the side door is open but no one is around.

"Weird," Garret mutters. "I know the farrier is supposed to swing by this morning but he always comes inside the clubhouse first so a brother or two accompanies him into the stables and yet no one is around. And it's afternoon, he should have been finished and out of here already."

I glance around me when Garrett takes out his phone and puts it to his ear, pulling me toward the stables to look inside. "Weston, didn't Seger leave yet? He was only here this morning, right? Why is his truck still—"

His voice is cut off at the same time Garrett spins around and roughly drags me out of the stables. I risk a glance over my shoulder and see a lifeless body on the floor.

"Oh, no," I gasp.

"Dead body in the stables, Nick still there?" Garrett grunts.

"Hang up," a voice snaps hard enough to make my heart jolt.

Garrett pulls me behind him and is no longer holding his phone when he growls, "Get the fuck out of here. This is private property and you're trespassing. Not to fucking mention there's a federal agent on our grounds who will arrest you on sight."

My fingernails dig into Garrett's leather cut while I risk a glance around him to watch my father point a gun at us.

"No," I snap, realizing he's here for me, for what he said he'd do and I can't let that happen. "I'll go with you, just let him go."

"Stay behind me, Raney," Garrett says with a load of domination and demand in his voice.

I take a step to the side but Garrett's arm swings back to keep me in place. A shot rings out and I scream as Garrett grunts.

"You're going to die slowly," Garrett snarls and I notice how his body is leaning to the side. Blood is soaking his pants and I realize my father must have shot him in the leg.

"This is none of your business. You bought a horse from me and nowhere in those papers or during the auction was mentioned you could freely fuck my daughter and make her a whore to do your bidding. It was a horse you bought, not a goddamn money cow along with it. Raney, get your ass in that van. Now." My father raises the gun and aims it at Garrett's head. "Or your fuckbuddy is going to get his brains mixed with the dirt underneath our feet."

"Big mistake coming here." I recognize the loud snapping voice as Weston's. "A bigger mistake to use the farrier as a cover to get in here unseen."

I glance behind me to see Roper, Weston, Oak, and a handful of other bikers standing next to each other.

"Private property, asshole. Look up and to your left and to your right. Hell, spin that fucking brainless head of yours three-sixty to see your little fuck-up has been documented. The security feed will send your ass to prison for a long damn time," Roper adds.

"You stole from me. I'm merely retrieving what's mine," my father bellows.

A man I don't know steps around the van and

is aiming a gun at my father. "I beg to differ, Wiley Bolcord. You see, the woman standing next to Garrett Verhams is a ghost. She has no birth certificate or social security number. And I'm sure if I ask her if she belongs to you or wants to go with you, she'll scream 'no fucking way.' Am I right, Raney?"

I'm stunned how this man I don't know seems to know all about me and weirdly enough stands up for me.

"Yeah," Harlene's voice flows through the air. "She's no one's property. Well, she's Garrett's property but he claimed her as his old lady, and that's different, so–"

"Too much rambling, Harlene." Cassidy cuts Harlene off and adds, "But she's right. Raney is our friend and no one will ever hurt her again."

"Or we'll kick your ass," Mayven growls and my eyes sting to see Muriel along with Greta and Kadence standing fierce behind the row of bikers.

Each and every one of Garrett's friends…no.

They have become my friends too in the short period of time I've been here. They are all standing up for me. They have my back while there's a man facing us with a gun in his hand. He just shot Garrett and can hurt a lot more people and it's all because of me.

This man standing before us might be my father but he only took things from me. He never cared anything about me. He only wanted the money I could make for him and the work I could do to help him.

He lied. He was cruel and not only in words but depriving me from a lot of things and basically robbed me of living. It was only when I got out from underneath his thumb when I realized he was basically suffocating the life out of me. It all ends here. I can't go with him because I just got a taste of how living is supposed to be.

"No fucking way," I say those words with my heart and soul. "I belong where I am, and that's right here on this ranch along with my friends and my old man."

My father's face turns furious and I've seen it many times. I know what's coming; his wrath. I try to push Garrett out of harm's way but not before a gunshot blasts through the air. My grip on Garrett fails when he launches forward and takes my father with him to the ground.

Another gunshot, and I watch how Garrett punches my father in the face. He's straddling him and lands one punch after another. I grab Garrett's leather cut and try to pull him off but it's useless.

"Stop. Please," I scream. "Please, Garrett, stop. I don't want you to end up in jail."

His brothers are surrounding us and manage to pull Garrett away. The man who I don't know but stood up for me anyway is kneeling down beside my father and is cuffing him.

"Don't worry, Raney. Garrett isn't the one going to jail, this fucker is."

I now assume this must be Nick, the one working for the FBI.

"Thank you," I croak and feel Garrett's strong arms surround me.

"Are you hurt?" His gaze slides over me.

Realization sets in. "You're hurt! He shot you. Someone call an ambulance."

"Already on its way," Harlene says as she rubs my back. "Come on, let the guys bring him inside so he can sit down and get his leg elevated instead of standing here in the dirt."

I step aside to allow Roper and Colt to each grab one of Garrett's arms to throw it over their shoulder as they balance his weight to get him to the clubhouse. I don't even give my father a second glance.

The people who I only met a little over a week ago mean more to me than a man who I have known all my life. Hell, strangers gave me more than he ever did and it's a hard contrast to balance my past and future. But I'm determined to put everything behind me and focus on a future where I'm in control of my own life.

We step inside the clubhouse and Joaquin comes rushing toward the couch where they are putting Garrett. He holds out a glass of water and places a medical kit on the table. Harlene and Cassidy both jump into action and pull on gloves before they cut open his jeans to assess the wound.

They might be vets but it's better than nothing. Hell, I don't even know what to do but they work together effortlessly to try to stop the bleeding and cover the wound. Sirens blare from outside and I release a deep breath when I finally see EMTs come rushing in.

Time passes where we head to the hospital to take out the bullet. He's so damn lucky from what I've heard. The bullet didn't do any real damage. But I heard more than one shot and it turns out one of those belonged to Nick who shot my father's hand in an effort to mess with his aim. Thankfully he did so when Garrett knocked them both to the ground, he wasn't shot.

He could have died.

I could have lost the man I love.

I know it might be too soon to talk or think about love but my heart and gut doesn't lie. What I feel for this man is beyond comparison. When you're wrapped with kindness, feel comfortable in silence to enjoy each other's company, share the same interest and passion in the hard work each of us does on the ranch; you know deep down it's a match made in heaven.

He is a slice of heaven right here on earth. My savior from the second I laid eyes on him. Everything feels right. And when you know what it's like when your body lights up at the sight of your man who is still alive and just woke up from a surgery to retrieve a bullet because he once again saved me from my father; you grab hold and never let go. You give meaning to that feeling and label it for what it is; love.

"Hey," he croaks and winces when he tries to sit up.

I carefully grab his hand and give it a squeeze.

"I was afraid I would lose you."

He gives me a faint smile. "Not a chance, sugar."

The door of Garrett's hospital room swings open and Decker stalks inside. "Is your lazy ass still in bed?"

"Shut up, asshole," Garrett grumbles.

"I just came in to let you know Raney's father is heading to jail and according to Nick it's an open and shut case with everything we have against him. He won't get out any time soon. And it's not just what that fucker did today but Nick also had a breakthrough with that other case. They–" His eyes go to me and he clears his throat. "Sorry, I can't tell it any other way than they did some kind of sonar thing when the dogs indicated they found something when they had a warrant to search the property. Nick is pretty sure they found a dead body buried on your dad's ranch. It must be from Ted since he's been missing and he did mention it to you. But we'll know more once they've recovered the body and such. We'll keep you up to date but I thought you guys would like to know everything is handled. He won't bother you again, Raney."

Tears are yet again sliding down my cheeks and I can't stop them. I'm not sad but they are happy tears.

"Thank you," I croak. "I'm so thankful to have all of you in my life."

Decker points a finger in my direction. "Meant to be and shit like that. You fit right in with the other old ladies and don't even mind the hard work around the ranch. And don't forget I placed an order, huh? You're damn good at braiding rope and I'm sure you know your father sold your stuff. You knew about that, right?"

I nod. "I knew he sold them. He had me sometimes make special orders."

"Well, you being the brains and actual hands behind those great items–" He cuts his sentence off and shoots me a wink. "You could sell them yourself. Make an online shop and get it up and running. You'll have a way to support you and do what you like for yourself. And I'm sure one of the guys can help you set up a website or anything else you need."

"Enough with the hints and tips. My woman is free to do what she wants, when she wants. Now go hunt down a doctor or nurse and ask when I can get my ass home," Garrett grunts.

Decker chuckles. "All right already. Don't go anywhere, I'll be right back."

Garrett curses while Decker's laughter fills the room as he heads in search for medical personnel.

"Come lie down next to me." Garrett scoots to the side.

I glance at his leg. "But you're wounded."

"Don't care, I need to feel you."

How can I ever deny him when I want the same thing? I carefully crawl into the bed with him and sigh in contentment. I want to tell him so badly about what I feel for him but I can't; it's too soon.

Lying in this bed and what we just went through might cause for him to think I'm telling him those words for different reasons.

But my heart skips a beat when he murmurs, "I fucking love your scent, your body against mine, and the way I feel when those bright green eyes of yours land on mine. I could say I love you but then you'd probably blame it on my dozed-up state. But I really do. You're so damn special. The second I laid eyes on you it was as if you jolted my body into awareness. And we now have the time to explore everything we want without having to look over our shoulder. Free to dream about a future, one where I do hope we have kids one day who also enjoy working with horses as much as we do."

"These days I can't seem to stop crying," I croak. "But I won't blame it on the medication because I love you too."

"Thank fuck. Shit. I don't think we can have sex today. Unless you ride me, that won't require me moving around as much."

A giggle escapes me. "We have all the time in the world and many positions and places to have sex. I have a feeling we won't ever grow tired of exploring things together."

He brushes his knuckles over my nipple. "I'm ready to start exploring when you are."

I gasp and jump off the bed when a nurse stalks into the room. Garrett chuckles and I shoot him a glare but it quickly turns into a smile when I remember what he just said, what we said to each other.

He loves me. He really, really loves me and offers me the world, one we built together with mutual respect and surrounded by friends. One where I will be sure to make my dream a reality. And I already have my knight in shining armor at my side.

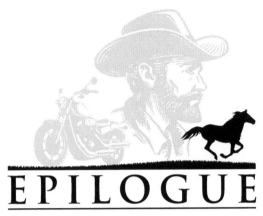

EPILOGUE

Two years later

GARRETT

I glance at the empty spot beside me and realize Raney isn't in bed with me. I don't know why but the memory of the first few days together two years ago assaults me. One where she would be restless and not able to fall asleep in bed and had to sneak out to the stables to sleep in the damn horse bedding with Izzy.

It changed the day I got out of the hospital. I have no clue if it was the change in life knowing she was completely freed from her father–since he's rotting in jail with a lifelong sentence–or her worry to make sure I was okay since I couldn't walk, let alone carry her back to bed like I did every day. Fact is, as of that day she slept in my arms every night.

Except now. But there's a logical explanation for it. I push myself up and notice my wife standing in front of the window, her eyes are glued on the darkness of the night. She has her hands on her back and she's twiddling with her wedding ring. I chose a golden band with a floral carved design and it looks very delicate around her finger.

"Any change?" I question.

She spins around and stalks back to the bed. "Did I wake you?"

I give a little shake of my head. "By standing silently by the window? Not a chance, sugar."

A tiny sigh flows over her lips and she slides between the covers to snuggle close.

"Fuck," I grunt at the feel of her cold feet brushing against my leg.

The giggle caressing my chest as she snuggles close is awakening my cock. Her hand slides over my abs and a moan tumbles from her when she wraps her fingers around my dick. I close my eyes and relish in her touch. Her mouth lingers on my neck, a sloppy kiss, making electricity dance over my skin.

After years she still manages to set my body aflame with desire while my heart holds hers. We share the same dreams and hopes, and it's for this reason we've only just decided it's time to take the next step in our future. Last night we threw all the condoms away and we're going to let fate decide if we get to expand our family.

And when I open my eyes and stare into hers–filled with the same amount of love and devotion as mine–I'd say we're more than ready to embrace any children we might be graced with. She's come a long way and is so damn strong and determined. She's managed to teach herself how to read with little help from me and her friends. She'll be a great mother. She's kind, loving, caring, devoted, overly protecting and I know all of this because I know her.

But mostly because Izzy is going to give birth any day and Raney has been sick with worry. It's the reason why she was standing in front of the window, keeping an eye on the stables while I'm sure she checked the feed of the camera we have set up to watch the mare.

I'm drawn out of my thoughts when Raney straddles me and places the head of my dick at her entrance, slowly sinking down to impale herself. I hold my breath and try to keep the tingle in my balls on a slow burn.

The sight above me is enthralling. Perfect tits peeking through her long black hair but it's her gorgeous green eyes that draw me in. We found love when we least expected it and were thrown into each other's path to move forward together; perfectly paired.

Her legs are on each side of me and I let my

hands slide up and over her hips to guide her movements. I break our stare because I have to watch how her pussy swallows my cock whole. Each time she moves up I get a glimpse of myself covered with her juices before I get tightly gripped by her walls, repeating the process over and over.

Confident enough she'll keep a delicious rhythm, I sneak one hand up to knead her breast and I tweak her nipple at the same time I let my thumb find her clit to draw small circles. Yeah, the desperate moan filling the air, along with the increasing squeezing of her pussy, is telling me she's close.

I lift my upper body and snatch her other nipple with my mouth, sucking hard and flicking it with my tongue while I hold it hostage between my teeth. Her fingers grip my head to keep me in place and she starts to fuck me. Rough. Riding me like there's no tomorrow and it makes my hips shoot off the mattress to meet her with the same ferocity.

Harsh breaths rip through the air, sweat coating

our bodies until my name is bouncing off the walls as she collapses on top of me to let her body surrender to the pleasure. I grip her hips and shamelessly use her limp body to grind myself as deep as I can to fill her up with my seed. Maximum intensity, maximum pleasure, and for sure as fuck; maximum love.

Our raging hearts try to settle but deep down they never will. They will always stay wild to chase the love flowing around us. A smile spreads my face while I let my hand slide over the back of her head.

The softness of her hair along with her warm breath flowing over my damp chest makes me damn happy. Though I know my woman is sated, she'd still have the restlessness flowing through her, the same when she was standing in front of the window.

And it's for this reason I ask, "Want to go check on Izzy?"

Her gorgeous head comes up and she stares at

me with a load of adoration. "You don't mind?"

"Woman," I grunt. "You know I'd bring her inside our bedroom if that makes you happy."

A smile falling right from heaven paints her face when she says, "Because you want me happy."

"Because you make me happy," I murmur and brush my lips against hers.

"Happy, loved, cherished, understood...I never knew something like this existed until you made me feel good the second I met you." The words are spoken with a load of emotion and slide like a straight arrow into my heart.

I feel the need to lighten the mood and the first thing that enters my brain is, "Let the good times roll, along with my hips to find the perfect spot inside you to make things forever roll our way."

Her head tips back and laughter flows from her body, making it shake so my dick slides out of her.

She glances down at me and murmurs, "Forever...*our way*."

"Fuck, yes," I rumble and fist her hair to keep her head in place to give her a kiss.

One where she knows I will keep the promise I just gave her; good times will sure as fuck keep rolling our way. And I can't wait to experience what the future holds for us as we realize our dreams with fulfilled hearts.

Esther E. Schmidt

THANK YOU!

Thank you for reading Garrett's story.
Gaining exposure as an independent author
relies mostly on word-of-mouth, so if you have
the time and inclination, please consider leaving
a short review wherever you can.
Even a short message on social media
would be greatly appreciated.

Be sure to check out all my other MC,
Mafia, Paranormal MC, and
Contemporary Romance series!
books2read.com/rl/EstherESchmidt

Signup for Esther's newsletter:
esthereschmidt.nl/newsletter

SPECIAL THANKS

My beta team;

Neringa, Tracy, Lynne, Judy, Tammi,

my pimp team, and to you, as my reader…

Thanks so much! You guys rock!

Contact:

I love hearing from my readers.

Email:

authoresthereschmidt@gmail.com

Or contact my PA **Christi Durbin**

for any questions you might have.

facebook.com/CMDurbin

ESTHER E. SCHMIDT

Visit Esther E. Schmidt online:

Website:

www.esthereschmidt.nl

Facebook - AuthorEstherESchmidt

Twitter - @esthereschmidt

Instagram - @esthereschmidt

Pinterest - @esthereschmidt

Signup for Esther's newsletter:

esthereschmidt.nl/newsletter

Join Esther's fan group on Facebook:

www.facebook.com/groups/estherselite

Join The Swamp Heads group on Facebook:

www.facebook.com/groups/TheSwampHeadsSeries

MORE BOOKS

COWBOY
BIKERS MC

MC

LOST VALKYRIES

THE DUDNIK CIRCLE

NEON MARKSMAN MC

PEACOCK

THE FAULTS OF OUR SINS

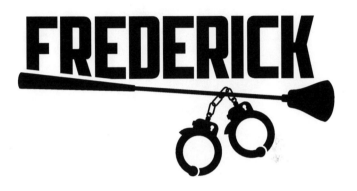

UNRULY DEFENDERS MC

UNRULY PROTECTOR

Swamp heads
SERIES

Made in the USA
Middletown, DE
25 November 2022

15982135R00116